If I Had Two Wings

If I Had Two Wings

Stories

Randall Kenan

W. W. NORTON & COMPANY

Independent Publishers Since 1923

For information about permission to reproduce selections from this
book, write to Permissions, W. W. Norton & Company, Inc.,
500 Fifth Avenue, New York, NY 10110

For information about special discounts for bulk purchases,
please contact W. W. Norton Special Sales
at specialsales@wwnorton.com or 800-233-4830

Manufacturing by LSC Communications, Harrisonburg
Book design by Lovedog Studio
Production manager: Julia Druskin

Names: Kenan, Randall, author.
Title: If I had two wings : stories / Randall Kenan.
Description: First edition. | New York : W. W. Norton & Company, [2020]
Identifiers: LCCN 2019050476 | ISBN 9781324005469 (hardcover) |
ISBN 9781324005476 (epub)
Subjects: LCSH: Angels—Fiction. | North Carolina—Social life
and customs—Fiction.
Classification: LCC PS3561.E4228 .A6 2020 | DDC 813/.54—dc23
LC record available at https://lccn.loc.gov/2019050476

W. W. Norton & Company, Inc., 500 Fifth Avenue, New York, N.Y. 10110
www.wwnorton.com

W. W. Norton & Company Ltd., 15 Carlisle Street, London W1D 3BS

1 2 3 4 5 6 7 8 9 0

For

JZKB and DJ
Godsons and nephews extraordinaire

Profound thanks to the Lannan Residency
Program in Marfa, Texas.

Two wings to veil my face.
Two wings to veil my feet.
Two wings to fly away,
and the world can't do me no harm.

—"Two Wings" [Traditional]

Contents

When
We All Get
to Heaven

New York City.

Ed Phelps was walking north up Seventh Avenue. He'd just come along 50th Street from seeing Rockefeller Center—just the way he remembered it, all spit-shined and brass-bright, the great big golden statue above the skating rink where they shot the *Today* show—and he wandered up the avenue, with no particular direction in mind. This was all after having splurged on a ten-dollar pastrami sandwich at the Carnegie Deli. His buddy Dr. Streeter had told him he would have to get one, and had relayed this information to Ed Phelps the way teenagers speak of sex or the way grandmothers speak of grandchildren. After having attacked the monstrous mound of spicy meat, Ed Phelps understood the good doctor's worship of said sandwich. And now he too would hold it in high esteem—it was indeed more than the sum of meat and bread and mustard and sour pickles.

He had left the deli happy, and continued in his delight as he walked about. Happy to be back in the metropolis after thirty years—was it thirty years? Had it been that long? Since he came back from Korea? He reckoned it to be true.

Ed stopped at a grocery stand where they displayed a fine selection of tomatoes, oranges, asparagus, apples of three—no, four—varieties, greens of all color and manner, and juices. And gladiolas and carnations—pink, red, white, yellow—and roses and a tall tower of water bottles, sweating and looking so very inviting on a hot summer day, the moisture drip, drip, dripping and condensing upon the bottles white like frost. The idea of actually paying for something that came free out of the tap bothered Ed, but he was sorely tempted to buy a bottle. He did not, ultimately, succumb.

As Ed stood and took in all the fare, this young fellow, who appeared to be Mexican, eyed Ed steadily. Ed smiled at the man. Of course Ed didn't know if the man was Mexican or not. But the man said not a word, nor did he blink. Ed continued to make miration at the fruits and vegetables and flowers, surprised to find such a fresh bounty available in the middle of New York. Lickety-split, right there on the street. He noticed the prices and shook his head. *Well, I reckon they damn well better be the finest apples in creation!*

Ed walked away, saying "Afternoon" to the Mexican fellow, who, again, did not blink.

But Ed was feeling good. Ed was feeling fine. Smack-dab in the middle of the rough-and-tumble of New York City, and no one paid him any more attention than they did to anybody else, and he was feeling safe and he was watching the people—so many people, stepping fast, on the move.

Ed and his wife, Isaline, were in town for the National Baptist Convention, being held at that very moment in the Javits Convention Center way, way over on Eleventh Avenue. Isaline was the delegate representing not only First Baptist

Church of Tims Creek, but her district of North Carolina. Ed was just tagging along. He was a trustee of the church, but not a deacon; Isaline was the mover and the doer of the family. She liked to call herself a people person. Ed thought it a wonder that she found the patience and the energy after all the time she spent fixing hair. She had just added a fifth chair to her beauty parlor, and putting in six days a week was the norm for her nowadays. But she said it made her happy to be doing and doing, and he believed her, and he had no intention of getting in her way, even when, from time to time, she took a bad mood and set to fussing about all she had to do, knowing she wasn't going to stop and just wanted him to rub her feet and acknowledge how much work she did, day in and day out, and tell her that she worked too darn hard and needed to slow down, knowing, of course, that slowing down was her last intention. Besides, every now and again being her husband took him places—for free—places like New York City, where he hadn't been in thirty? . . . Twenty-nine? . . .

The noise worked like a tonic. He didn't remember the noise. Cars. Trucks. Horses and buggies. Jackhammers. Horns. Shouts. Rumblings coming up from under the ground. Mysterious hisses. Cranes in the sky. Barking dogs. Folk hollering. Crying babies. Horns and more horns.

He saw a woman dressed like the first lady step over a bum without even hesitating. He saw a man in a fine-looking business suit and fine shoes throwing up in the gutter, right there in the middle of the street. A man walked up to Ed and handed him a pink slip of paper. "You look like you could use the downtime," the dark-skinned man said under his mirror shades, giving Ed a schoolboy grin. On the card was the outline of a woman with bodacious proportions, front and back, and the legend read—in pink—New York's Most Sophisticated Pussy. Ed dropped this in the next trash can he saw, embarrassed at the prospect that somebody might have seen him handling it.

But Ed's spirits were still high, and he looked all about him, and most people—white, brown, yellow—were just stepping. He liked that. He liked to see the haste and the fast movements, people on their way somewhere. Where were they going? Lord knows, but they were aiming to get there. In a hurry.

And Ed was feeling good. He was stepping. He was happy and dandy and fine.

Plumbing was Ed Phelps's trade and he had done well. After he came back from overseas at twenty-seven, he settled on pipes. His daddy had said, *Folk always gone need somebody to fix they pipes.* He got a job working for Old Man Yancey Carter for a while, who was a white fellow, but a fair fellow. He next took a job down at Camp Lejeune. When he found out that the government would pay for courses, he took classes in plumbing at Owen Cross Community College in the seventies, and, by and by, he was working for himself. Today he had three people working for him, and he had no complaints. No sir. Put two girls through college. Was prepared to put a boy through, too, but Edmund wound up going to the Air Force Academy, which made Ed proud.

Ed walked up Seventh Avenue to Central Park South and strolled over to Columbus Circle, where he beheld the statue at the entrance to the park, a monument to the *Maine*—he had seen that on the Discovery Channel—all doused in pigeon doo-doo, but that didn't stop the young folk from sitting all around its base. He stood for a spell watching the scruffy teenagers on their skates—the kinds that look like ice skates with wheels—and it made him smile. He watched one woman for a particularly long while—she must have been Puerto Rican with her light caramel skin and long jet-black hair and a body that brought to mind a fawn—her movements were a thing of beauty to Ed Phelps, and he didn't want to look away, but he didn't want to stare either, so he walked on.

Feeling fine.

Ed Phelps was two years shy of his sixtieth birthday, and he could say in all honesty that he had no notion of retiring. Ed's own daddy had worked—out in the hot fields—till he was eighty-eight, and Ed planned to go at least that long. Besides, he was in good health. He'd given up the cigarettes now on ten years. Isaline watched his diet like a hawk. Doctor said his cholesterol was low. And his heart was as strong as a buffalo's.

Ed thought about walking up into the park, to see that bridge over that pond that's in every other movie about New York, along with the Sheep Meadow, and that pond where little toy children play with little toy boats, but he looked at the time and figured he should begin to make his way back to the convention center. The day before, he had sat around with Isaline, attended the opening ceremony and a few panels, but today Isaline was in meetings, and Ed really didn't want to just sit around. He didn't feel like going back to his hotel either—they were staying at the Milford Plaza—so he continued walking.

He wore that day the suit Isaline had bought him for his

fifty-fifth birthday—and it still fit—along with a red tie his son Edmund had given him for Christmas. And though it seemed most men these days didn't bother with hats, he fancied his black wide-brim and kept it on his head.

At 53rd Street, for no particular reason, Ed decided to turn west again. He was feeling fine. Adventuresome even. Enjoying his walk. Enjoying the way the air in New York smelled, all full of car exhaust, cooking food, sewer gas, garbage, and perfume.

Ahead of him—about mid-block—he saw a large group of young people, mostly white folk, gathering. Why, he did not know. Part of him knew he should go across the street, but—feeling adventuresome as he did—he kept on toward the group to investigate.

Boys and girls mostly they were, dressed casually in their T-shirts and jeans. He did, however, notice a lot of the T-shirts bore the same likeness of a man with spiky hair and the word "Billy" and something else he couldn't quite decipher, but Ed Phelps had no idea who or what he was, and decided right away that he didn't care. This was fun. This was a lark. In a few days he'd be back in Tims Creek snaking out septic lines.

As he waded through the throng—which he now saw was only about twenty or thirty people—and saw they were waiting for somebody, obviously, to show, probably coming out of that door there, he set his mind—"Excuse me, please. 'Scuse me. Pardon me"—to getting through to the other side of the crowd.

A white stretch limousine pulled up at that moment (a Lincoln, Ed Phelps took note), and the crowd of which Ed was now plumb in the middle began to buzz like a hive of hornets. A door flung open and two leggy white women dressed—barely—in one-piece black outfits that left not one thing to the imagination except the color of their pubic hair, emerged from the car. Following them was a much shorter man—the one with the hair standing straight up in the air, all blond like hoarfrost and needle-looking, like a porcupine, or like a man who had stuck his finger into a light socket and saw God all at the same time.

The man chewed gum and had a sneer about his face, and quickly slipped on a pair of dark shades. He certainly didn't dress like a man who rides around in limousines. He wore a black leather jacket over a T-shirt that was shredded, showing his pale underbelly, and his pants were like vinyl—but Ed quickly thought better and figured they had to be leather, and next reckoned that those pants had to be mighty hot on a day like today, even if you were riding around in the back of a limousine. And though the man did not in the least look happy to see this score and more of eager young people, they certainly were—without a doubt—happy to see him—"Billy! Billy!"

The doors to the building swung wide and three gorilla-sized men rushed out to push the crowd back, creating a path between this Billy man and the door. It just so happened that Ed Phelps stood at that path, just like the adoring fans. Ed couldn't remember the last time he had felt so aware of his own presence, and so embarrassed to be somewhere. Though he had to admit it was a little exciting. Something to report on when he got back home.

As the Billy man and the four legs attached to two women walked through the path the three men had created, the crowd grew louder, reaching out with posters of this Billy and compact discs and albums and little books and pens.

At this point, almost by design, Ed and Billy were standing face-to-face—it was a mere flash of a second, a moment in time, before one of the human oxen came to push Ed Phelps to the side and sweep Billy into the brick building.

Billy snatched off his sunglasses, stuck his arms up and out wide, and hollered: "Deacon!" This ejaculation caused nearly everyone to pause—the two long-legged women, the three grizzly-bear security men, a quantity of the nearby crowd—and Ed Phelps. Before Ed could say—what?—Billy made a kingly motion to the Three Muscle-teers, and everyone—Billy, the women, and Ed—were swept into the back of the building.

Oh hell, Ed thought, *what am I going to do now?*

The hallway itself was dim and dingy and narrow, and Ed had no choice but to follow along with the pack, as he was in their midst. Directly they came to a larger room. The door was open and several people, some in suits and some in nice dresses, lolled about, but perked up when Billy walked through the door. The back wall was one long mirror above a long table full of bottles and jars and brushes and tubes. Goose-egg lightbulbs ran all along the top.

"Francesca!" Billy said to a woman dressed all in black. He kissed her on both her cheeks and gave her a third peck as if for good measure.

She said, "Billy," once, and kissed at his cheek—not touching it—only once. She did not smile. Her eyes had a fish-like flatness that made Ed Phelps uneasy.

"This," Billy said, and made an extravagant flourish with his hand, "this is the Deacon." He had an accent like one of those Beatles, or some of those British people on those PBS shows Isaline liked to watch sometimes, and not the rich and fancy kind, more like the kind who drove trucks and worked in butcher shops. And at that very moment it was quite clear to Ed Phelps that Billy was winking at him, his back turned to the Francesca lady. To be sure, this Billy fella was up to something and wanted Ed to be in on it. But the question was: Was he up to good or to no good? Ed Phelps would just have to hang out to find out.

"Francesca Eberhardt here, Deacon, is my A & R person. She's an executive with my label. She gives things the ups and the downs, the green lights, the red lights, the yellow lights, the black lights—d'you know what I mean?—I mean she's a real, real, real powerful bitch. And my fate is in her hands, innit?"

Francesca said not a word. She simply stared at Billy with her rattlesnake eyes. She was dressed in a black dress that could have been spray-painted on her swamp-weed frame. Her long, inky hair was pulled back, making her face look even more gaunt and pale against all that black.

"You see, Francesca here has a BA in economics from Stanford, an MBA from Harvard—was it Harvard, love? Yes, Harvard—and a PhD from the London School of Economics, but, funny thing—she don't know nothing about no music. It's a riot, innit?"

"Billy," Francesca finally said, her voice a bit warmer than Ed Phelps would have expected, but chilly nonetheless. "If this is about your contract, I assure you—"

"Me contract? Me contract? Fuck the bloody contract."

Francesca pointed a long and well-sculptured finger at

Billy: "Look, my friend, I can put up with a lot of your crap, but there will be no fucking of any contracts. Don't you fuck with me. You belong to me now. Capiche?"

This brief lecture seemed to achieve the desired effect upon everyone in the room, all of whom were looking at their feet, to windows, to doors, away from eyes—all, that is, except for Billy.

"Belong? Did you say belong? I mean how insensitive can you be?" Billy thrust his hands toward Ed. "I mean, really—*belong*? We call that bad form where I'm from, missy."

It came upon Ed that he would be expected to hold forth on this development, and the idea sat with him not at all well, and he began to look for a way out of this prickly situation.

"I bet you don't even know the Deacon's music, do you, Francesca?"

"Well," she said, "to be honest, I—"

"Well, of course you don't. I mean, how old are you? Sixteen? Miss Stanford, Miss Harvard MBA, Miss I-actually-prefer-Mahler—Jesus Christ! Can you fucking believe she actually said that to me?"

"Mussorgsky, actually. I said, Mussorgsky, not Mahler."

Billy began to close in on Francesca, and in turn wagged his finger at her: "The Deacon is a legend, young lady. The Deacon and His Hounds of Hell. From Hell. They were fantastic—I saw them in Berlin in 1972 . . ."

After turning to one of his long-legged assistants ("Give us a fag, eh, darling?") and lighting up, he launched into a long, detailed story about how Ed/the Deacon had grown up on a plantation in Mississippi, and had run away to Memphis at the age of twelve, and how he had run into a great big chicken at the same crossroads as had Robert Johnson ("You do know who Robert Johnson is, don't you, darling? Yeah, I thought you might not"), and how he got a recording contract with Sam Phillips and then Chess Records—and Ed Phelps couldn't keep up with the story, but found it so very compelling that he wanted to hear this man's music until it hit him—making him laugh—that he was, indeed, this very man. Lord, this boy could tell a good lie. Ed more than halfway admired that.

His cigarette almost done, Billy took a long draft followed by a long pause. His eyes seemed even darker and more impish. Francesca let out a big sigh and looked at her watch. Billy walked over to a corner, smoke flowing like fog from his nostrils, and picked up a case and put it on a table. He undid the latch and the top gave a slight creak open. A guitar. Of course. Just wood and wire. Billy ran a finger over it and looked directly at Ed Phelps. Ed Phelps beheld the guitar and he beheld Billy. He wanted to shake his head, *No*, but something about the entire situation tickled him, and he grinned despite himself. Billy himself grinned right back at him. It might have looked as if the two of them were drunk.

"Deacon," he said, with a rather studied deference: "Would you be so kind as to play for us?"

Oh hell. Ed Phelps wondered how things had come to this particular pass.

At that moment, between them, something odd and familiar occurred: two boys who together and without words recognize and acknowledge the Dangerous Thing, and, being like-minded, imagine assaying said Thing, and with each passing moment feel the Thing exert greater gravitational force upon the two, each to each, and along with the weight comes glee, anticipation, heat, so much so that the Dangerous Thing becomes the Irresistible Thing, the Inevitable Thing.

Ed Phelps picked up the guitar and began to strum. As he tuned the instrument, a look of quietness and acute observation overtook Billy's face, very like a cat.

The tuning did not take too terribly long, and, truth to tell, though Ed Phelps had not picked up a guitar in over fifteen years, and had probably forgotten more than he had ever known, as he strummed and hummed to himself, doorways in the back of his mind began to slowly open, then more and more, one by one, two by two, four by four, and he remembered his grandfather and how he played and how he taught Ed to play, and he remembered playing on the back porch with Mr. Moses Rascoe, who drove a truck, but who was so good he played sometimes for money, and like a silverfish under a sink, a song jumped up into Ed Phelps's head and he commenced to sing and play:

You get a line and I'll get a pole, honey.
You get a line and I'll get a pole, babe.
You get a line and I'll get a pole,
We'll go fishin' in the crawdad hole.
Honey, baby mine.

Ed Phelps looked all about and Billy's face was no longer cat-like, but all Christmas, and all the young people in the room were beaming and tapping their feet—with the logical exception of Francesca, who looked as if she might bite him at any second.

He remembered a verse that Mr. Moses had taught him:

What did the catfish say to the eel, honey?
What did the catfish say to the eel, babe?
What did the catfish say to the eel?
The more you wiggle, mama, the better I feel,
Honey, baby mine.

Ed Phelps put an end to the song with a sweet ping and a run that brought back blueberry-pie memories. Billy rose, and was full of whoops and hollers and hot praise, and his friends and folk were clapping, and Billy set in straightaway figuring how he could get Ed up onstage with him.

"Oh hell, no," Francesca said.

"Seriously, it'll be a riot," Billy said.

"Well," Ed said, "I have to meet the wife in a little bit anyway."

"Oh," Billy said, "she won't mind. We can invite her. It'll be a riot."

"I. I would mind, Billy." Francesca was now standing in front of Billy, towering over him, upon her face the expression of the schoolteacher who has finally reached her limit: "He can stay. He can watch the show. He can even bring little Mrs. Deacon and his hellhounds for all I care. But he is not going up on that stage with you, bubba. You dig? Fuck not with me, kiddo. Now—I believe you have a show to do, and I promised you'd be on time. For a change." Francesca walked out the door.

As soon as Francesca left the room, Billy embraced Ed Phelps, kissed him on the cheek, and said, "Thank you, mate.

You're a real trouper." He introduced Ed to his two assistants, saying they would take care of all his needs and that he'd see him after the show.

Ed did not realize that all this time he was in a theater called the Ritz, and he was ushered up into a VIP box to overlook the standing crowd and the stage. One of Billy's assistants led him to a phone where he left a message for Isaline, that he wouldn't be able to join her for *Les Misérables* but he was all right and he'd see her after the show.

After a long, long time, the lights went down and the music finally began. Ed Phelps was at once excited and deflated. He was happy to be here, happy to be a VIP, but he did not particularly care for the music, which made him a little sad. It was silly music, it was loud music, it was all catchy phrases and easy beats, stuff he heard on the radio, and he figured he might have heard some of this music on the radio in the past, but, to tell the truth, it all kinda sounded the same these days. But the young people seemed to enjoy the music, and they seemed to enjoy Billy, and this made him happy.

Billy himself came off as a rough boy, a rude boy, a loud boy, a dirty boy, a tough boy. All of which made Ed Phelps laugh. He wondered how Billy would have done in the navy. There were some mighty tough men there, and a lot of them were even smaller than Billy, and they did not wear leather.

During the intermission, Francesca came up to him and shook his hand. She did not have a smile on her face, but she did seem more pleasant. "You never played guitar professionally a day in your life, did you?"

"Ah, well, no, ma'am. You are correct."

"He thinks I'm an idiot, but you don't get to be senior

executive vice president at thirty for not knowing music. I know music."

"Yes, ma'am."

❈

AFTER THE CONCERT, he found his way back to the green-room, and to the assistants. He wanted to thank Billy, but didn't want to take up any more of his time. So he asked the assistants to thank Billy for him, and he donned his hat and headed for the door, on his way back to the Milford Plaza and to Isaline.

Just as he reached the outside door, he heard Billy calling, his boots tapping against the floor.

"Deacon, my friend, a bunch of us are going down to Bobby De Niro's new place. Would you please be my guest? You'll love it. It'll be a riot!"

Ed Phelps thought on it, thought about what he would say to Billy and these young people, thought about the senior executive vice president and music he didn't respect.

"Thank you kindly. And you have been awful kind. But I need to get back with my wife. She may think I'm laying dead in a gutter somewhere."

"All right, my friend. I can dig it. At least let me drop you off. Where are you staying?"

❈

JUST BILLY AND Ed in the backseat, and as soon as they sat down Billy launched into a long discussion of his career and the music business these days, and how he was once on top, and then the bitch hit him, sent him in a spiral, how you always need to look out for the bitch because the bitch is jealous . . . and Ed was beginning to have a difficult time following him, and couldn't figure if the bitch was the music industry, a woman, or just life, and he didn't really care. The leather seats were deep and plush, and he couldn't help but admire the scenery as the large car glided through the streets of Manhattan, and his mind wandered as Billy carried on . . .

The men, the women, the girls, the boys, all well lit in the nighttime, but accompanied now by long shadows, the bikes weaving in and out of traffic, the hot dog carts, the ambulances and flashing police cars, the subway entrances issuing forth human after human like ants from a mound, the streetlamps and the blinking colored lights, above stores and offices, the giant words crawling across buildings that told the world news, and the giant head twenty stories high or more, saying, obviously, something of grand importance, but at the same time nothing nowhere could be as important as being there right there, right then in all that color and size and flash . . .

By and by, the car came to a stop, and the driver got out and opened the door for Ed. He turned to Billy and said, "Can I ask you something?"

"Shoot."

"How did you know I could play a little guitar?"

"I didn't, mate. I had this feeling though. Call it me intuition. I figured if you couldn't you'd just tell me to fuck off, or something like that, innit? Just having a laugh."

They shared a chuckle. As he was getting out Billy asked his name.

"Ed. Ed Phelps of Tims Creek, York County, North Carolina."

"Ed." Billy stuck out his hand and shook Ed's. "Very pleased to make your acquaintance, Ed Phelps of North Carolina."

The walk to his hotel room took a while, the hall of the Milford Plaza being long and skinny and harshly bright.

When he got to the room he found Isaline in the tub—he called to her, and opened the bathroom door, and saw nothing but mist and was hit in the face by a wall of heat so thick and by the scent of pomegranate and strawberry and God-knows-what, all of which quickly took his breath away—

"Close that door, man! Don't you let out my heat!"

I will never understand, he thought, *why this woman insists on turning her nightly bath into a sauna*, but left her to her devices, glad to finally be home. He'd tell her all about his day when she got out, which could be in thirty minutes, which could be an hour.

He put on his pajamas—the fancy silk paisley pair Edmund had given him for Christmas—much too fancy for his tastes and much, much too fancy to wear every day, but they seemed appropriate for this trip. He got into bed and waited for Isaline. The TV was on, the sound cut down, playing some Lifetime TV drama she was forever watching. Ed took hold of the remote and commenced to flip through the channels, hoping to find the Hitler Channel or Discovery.

Something caught his eye and Ed Phelps paused and there he was. He looked tiny there on the screen and much younger than he had just a while ago, and so very white, all that white hair against such glowing white skin. He looked downright sick and pitiful. He looked like he needed to go home to his mama and get something good to eat.

He was singing one of the songs he had sung earlier that very evening, the song about dancing with himself, and Ed Phelps still couldn't make heads nor tails of it, and figured it meant something dirty, but just didn't care to know, nor did he care for the beat, which was monotonous and straightforward and boring—and oh my Lord . . .

In the music video—which made even less sense than the song—all these white folk who were supposed to be zombies or homeless people or such, in either event scary-looking, he supposed—though they couldn't have scared a baby goldfish even if they tried hard—were climbing up this tall, tall, tall skyscraper to get at Billy, who was singing about masturbation or whatever up on the roof of this building. There are puppets and all kind of random foolishness thrown in . . . and at the very end, Billy grabs ahold of some electrode-looking thing and becomes electricity and shoots bolts of lightning at the pretty zombies and they all fall down to earth, from the supertall building, and Billy continues to go on about how he wants to dance with himself, and Ed Phelps is left to wonder about so many things. And the day makes more sense and the day makes less sense, and he is happy to be in bed, and have it all to think about, all to tell about, to Isaline, to Dr. Streeter, and he must remember to tell Isaline about the pastrami sandwich at the Carnegie Deli . . .

The day weighed down upon him, but the day was feather-soft, the day was sweating bottles of water, the day was loud like cigars and smelled of truck horns, the day was a golden giant flying among the skyscrapers delivering fire to a beautiful Latina—*Oye mamá! Oye mamá-sa!*—hot day, long day, sweet day, music day, and the day turned to a guitar and the guitar strings turned to worms and the worms turned into cucumbers and the cucumbers turned into his mother's fingers, and she gave them to him peeled white with salt and pepper and a little vinegar, and the taste was childhood, and the taste was still new, and the sun was high in the sky, and it was 1946 and he was fourteen, and he was in the tobacco field, and deep in the lugs, and the day was hot, but he was happy—BACCOOO! BACCOOO! AIN'T NO BACCO IN HEAVEN I KNOW!—and he heard his grandfather's voice, and his grandfather was singing, and he heard his grandfather's voice and his grandfather was singing.

I Thought
I Heard the
Shuffle of
Angels' Feet

From the beginning I found the American male to be so alluring. They are like children, even the old ones. The fear of their own feelings gives them such magnetism. They do not seem to realize that such avoidance makes them that much more vulnerable. Open.

—*From Pixote, with Love,*
Jacson Ribeiro

"Goddamn Lexus." It was Jacson's car. Not Cicero's style. Too big, too expensive, too much a "statement." Jacson has been all about statements. His life was a statement. As had been his death.

Now Cicero Cross sat in a dead luxury car in the middle of a York County gravel road, watching the rain come tum-tum-tumbling down. This storm was like the storms Cicero remembered from his youth—great late-afternoon deluges accompanied by a preternatural darkness, great crashes of lightning, nature's resounding timpani of thunder. He remembered his grandmother saying: "Hush now, boy. God is talking."

He was actually shocked when his cell phone got a signal. This being Down East, North Carolina, where he got no reception fifty percent of the time. This being one of those perfect movie moments when our hero runs out of options, his back against the wall. Caught out in the rain. And here comes the monster . . .

The nice Mumbai voice at AAA, so machine-pleasant, unhurried, empathetic, full of guileless cheer, told him a truck was on the way and would be there to pick him up in forty-five minutes to an hour. Maybe a little longer. Cicero felt a bit miffed that it would take so long, then relaxed into that sense of release: no longer in his hands. Help is on the way. He regretted that he couldn't listen to the radio. Five hundred specialty stations beamed down with Arthur C. Clarke-blessed electromagnetism; blanketing the planet; a perfect time to listen to all-Sinatra or all-Sly and the Family Stone or all-Barbara Walters. But only the pelting of H_2O and his thoughts, his guilt, to keep him company. At least it wasn't midwinter.

"Fucking goddamn Lexus."

The lights appeared surprisingly soon, in less than twenty minutes. A dark figure, rather hulking, swung out and down from the high door with simian agility, and Cicero got out in the rain to meet his savior. The rain was just mizzle now, faint and soft. He could smell the cornfield to his left, and the cotton field to his right.

"Hey, boy," Tony said.

"Tony? That you? I . . . damn."

Tony Carter reached out his great paw, calloused and hard. "Been a while, ain't it?"

"Man, am I glad to see you. This damn car just shut down on me. Can't get a peep out of it."

"Let's hook her up and take her in and we'll see about getting you on the road."

Cicero stood back and watched his old high school classmate—how long had it been? Fifteen years? Twenty years? Tony Carter maneuvered the high and wide wrecker, backing it up to the front of the car, lowering the mechanism, chaining the wheels, slowly, deliberately lifting up the overpriced hunk of glass and steel and chrome and rubber like a casket.

Tony had been a big guy, back in the day, now he was huge, heavyset, but, as they say, he wore it well. He still moved with the grace of the athlete he once was, and still had that reserve which made his stillness, in contrast to his speed, disquieting. And thrilling.

"Go ahead and get in the truck, man, we're about ready to roll."

In the cab of the truck Tony stopped before he started down the road and beamed at Cicero, full face, the way a relative looks at a soldier home from war. "Good to see you, bro."

HIS UNCLE said Cicero wanted to sell his land. He was right. But not for the reasons Dax Cross thought.

"Boy, you ain't selling shit. If you and Tisha Ann agree to sell that land after I'm dead and gone, then you won't have my blessing, but you'll be free to do it. But I'll be goddamned if I let you sell it while I got breath in my body."

The coughing commenced. Red-eyed and rheumy, Dax Cross was now so emaciated and ashen, his coughs thoroughly wracked his body. The smells that wafted up and down the halls of the Seraphim Care Assisted Living reminded Cicero of his grandmother. Liniment oil. The same brand, no doubt. But there were other smells, the antiseptic kind, the all-too-human kind, the smell of cafeteria carrots and Salisbury steak and instant mashed potatoes and peas and Jell-O served in Styrofoam boxes for those too weak to hobble down the hall, like his uncle, who no longer had the heart to battle with his wheelchair. "One hundred acres left. One hundred. I inherited that from my granddaddy, and he inherited it from his daddy. Got another fifty acres from RuthEster. Hated to sell that. And told myself . . ."

His uncle had been repeating this story to Cicero for over a year now. Starting when he and his cousin Tisha Ann decided, after the amputation, that Dax Cross couldn't stay at home alone any longer. Dax fought the idea even when it became apparent, even to him, that the cost of completely refurbishing the eighty-year-old house they had all grown up in to accommodate an electric wheelchair, to refit the bathroom, the ramps, the lights—even with the government assistance—would be too expensive. Tisha Ann agreed. For the first forty-seven years of Cicero's life, Dax Cross had been a firm but cheerful older man, philosophical, even-tempered. In fact Cicero could not remember his uncle ever raising his voice except when Cicero was a boy and had done something extraordinarily foolhardy, like let the dog in the chicken coop, or leave the refrigerator door wide open all night. But for the last year he had become a constant, screaming, yelling, cussing, fiery pain; it was as if diabetes had stolen not only his leg but his sense of himself. Instead of sadness, Dax Cross seemed only to experience anger.

"I got my army pension. I got my teacher's pension. I got my TIAA-CREF. I'll be damned if I'm gonna sell that land."

"We can keep the house, Dax. But—"

"*But* my black ass, you fucking Nazi faggot. Get the hell outta here! Go. I'm sick of looking at you. You fucking asshole. Talking about selling my land."

"Uncle Dax. I—"

"Get the fuck out I said!"

The nurse, a gentle-faced white woman, her hair in a stylish brush cut, who seemed not in the least pained to intervene, placed her hand on Cicero's shoulder. "We better let your uncle rest now, son. He's been having trouble resting. Ain't that right, Mr. Cross?"

Dax Cross leered at the woman, combination vampire and werewolf. "I am not a child. Don't talk to me like I'm a fucking baby."

"Language, language, Mr. Cross! Or I'll spank you!" She gave an ineffectual and out-of-place giggle.

"Okay, Dax. I'm going to go now. Need to get back to Washington."

"Yeah. Right."

The nurse walked Cicero to the front desk. She gave him warm and fuzzy platitudes about how the loss of mobility can make amputees feel helpless and defensive, how worsening blood sugar levels can affect the emotions of severe diabetics. Cicero had heard it all before, and, in truth, felt no guilt over what he had to do. But that did not make him feel peachy.

> When I arrived in Vermont it was January. The
> temperature was 2 degrees below zero. In my mind
> I cursed the kindly priest who had sent me here.
> I thought I was in hell. I was very angry with this
> Jesus person who had delivered me from evil.
>
> —*From Pixote, with Love,* Jacson Ribeiro

Jacson loved to take the piss out of men like Justin Harbinson, who wasn't a dot-com billionaire as non-business reporters sometimes misidentified him. Harbinson had made his money in telephony software, essentially, in a series of programs that revolutionized wireless communications; the Baby Bells doted on him the way the wise men doted on the Christ child; and then—after he had semiretired at the tender age of twenty-nine, selling his first hatchling for an amount of money that could sustain a small country for a couple of years—he went into the gaming industry with the lust of a teenager after a *Playboy* model. Now Harbinson wanted their firm, R+C², to build his tomb. The image of a church they designed in Eatonville, Florida, published in *Fortune* magazine, had captured his imagination. It felt, he told Jacson, kinda Zen. He had said to himself, that day, Justin Harbinson did, that Jacson Ribeiro was the man who would build his mausoleum. Harbinson was thirty-six and, as far as anyone knew, as healthy as a sperm whale.

Rather than one big house, Justin Harbinson's estate, situated just north of Sonoma Valley, was a compound: five houses of vaguely Japanese (twelfth-century) design. His true extravagance and passion was reserved for the grounds, "Zen" through and through: Zen rock gardens, Zen fountains, Zen bridges. Too much Zen if you asked Cicero, especially considering that (a) Justin Harbinson had no visible religion, having grown up unchurched in a Cleveland suburb, and was now ostensibly agnostic or even atheist, but certainly not a Buddhist; and (b) there really wasn't any such thing as Zen architecture or Zen design. It was the sort of excess of moderation that made Cicero's teeth cringe.

Normally, R+C^2 turned down celebrity work. Or at least Jacson had. A few rich and famous souls had enticed him by tacking on worthy projects; footing worthy bills; he suckered one Southern-belle superstar into building an entire orphanage in Pinpoint, GA, in exchange for the design of a guesthouse that nobody would ever see, really, but that gave her bragging rights. The sicker Jacson got, the more perverse he became about such deals. "Baby, you just need to tell the man no," Cicero had told his lover.

"Why? He has promised to endow a school. Right here in Washington. No? This is good, no? Of course. He's a big man. A very big man—" The rue that crossed Jacson's face had grown less mischievous and more hateful as he grew weaker, thinner. His great frame ever more skeletal. "He wants a great lasting monument to mark his inconsequential life. No? So be it. He can afford it. No? Besides. He's so cute. I love to look upon his lovely, pure face while it spouts such bullshit."

THEY HAD known each other as undergraduates, but had not dated. Cicero knew of Jacson; everyone did. Jacson was ashamed to admit, later, that he did not remember Cicero when they were reunited almost ten years after they had graduated.

Back in their Howard University days, Jacson had been much too busy. Already a social butterfly, a force of nature, a legend in the making. Six foot six inches of beige, Portuguese-accented brawn, the Brazilian wunderkind. He moved like a dancer, he spoke like a poet—and Americans are such suckers for accents. Born for the world of design, even as an undergraduate he had developed his own style: the colorful

African fabrics that he wound about his sinewy frame like royal raiments; the jewelry, which on a man even slightly less herculean would have made him look like a drag queen, but on Jacson Ribeiro appeared not only regal but somehow manly. Shaved head. Nose ring. Gleaming white teeth. Eyes dark as caverns. He never slept alone. Cicero joined the crowd of all those who pined after the majestic Brazilian. I hear he's dating that guy from that television show. You know the one. Oh, really? I heard he's sleeping with that movie actress. Naw, I saw him with the son of the ambassador from Brunei. They were like *this*. Seriously.

Famously the wretched child of the wretched streets of indifferent Rio de Janeiro. Famously abandoned by his father. Famously not knowing who his mother had been. Famously selling his body and stealing to survive. Famously encountering a Catholic priest on a mission to save the youth of Brazil. Famously spirited away to New England at the volatile age of fourteen. Famously taken in by a retired physicist and his high school guidance counselor wife. Famously something of a physical giant at seventeen. Famously gay. Famously brilliant. Famously ambitious. Famously gifted at self-promotion. Jacson Ribeiro didn't know a damn thing about capoeira until he, as a high school student in Vermont, witnessed a traveling troupe in Stowe—rippling, multihued stallion-like bodies, flipping, kicking, soaring, bending: the lyricism of manliness, the prosody of testosterone unbound, the dance of the Brazilian soul. He had felt an ex-patriot's true pride for the first time; he was hooked. But the myth that he had learned it as a boy in the streets of Rio de Janeiro was one of those legends he allowed to blossom. Even when he set the record straight in his memoir, *From Pixote, with Love*, the idea persisted, seemed to cling to his massive body, as if the muscles and the smile and the jewels spoke their own truth: reality be damned.

Ten years. Cicero went on to get an MS in structural engineering, but found designing oil derricks and superstores and factories to be a dull thing. When his cousin invited him to join her architectural firm, he found he reveled in architectural school, in the history of building and design, in houseness, in the beauty and philosophy of edifice, and was delighted to become the second C in C+C—Cross and Cross, Architects. But it was his cousin Isadore's idea to link up with this up-and-coming architect who was winning awards and setting new standards and causing such a stir with his "exotic" postmodern blends of Arab and Spanish and Southern American designs; his cutting-edge use of technology, found materials, and social and environmental consciousness—an architect for the times, and such a dazzling showman to boot. Already his name was included in the same sentences as Gehry and Johnson and Mockbee. Promise incarnate. Jacson Ribeiro? Yeah, we went to school together. Isadore had worked with Jacson when he first got out of architectural school at a large Chicago firm where he first made his bones. She marveled at his panache, his verve, his inventiveness and dash and chutzpah and disregard for the status quo. They had remained friends.

Of course he'd been following Jacson's career from afar. One of those benchmarks one uses to measure one's own life. Thirty-three and are you happy? Is this all there is? Two long-term relationships with a dutiful doctor and a patient music teacher had left Cicero wary of matters of the heart. Isadore's eager plan to hire Jacson meant nothing to him, other than the sure understanding that Cicero would be needed for his knowledge of stress fractures and balance loads, and not for his deep appreciation for Florentine design of the sixteenth century.

"Has Atlas shrugged yet?" was the first thing Jacson said to him that day he came into the office, dressed like a Mauritanian bedouin, hooded in indigo silks as lush as a pasha's, his gold and platinum bracelets jangling, turquoise and lapis lazuli rings sparkling, as he shook Cicero's hand. That damned smile. Fucker.

> Despite what has been said in the press, I began
> to study capoeira as a freshman at Howard University. My first teacher was a black Puerto Rican
> master named Umberto, and my first real lover.
> But it was the beginning of my appreciation for
> the tradition that poverty in the urban slums had
> barred from me, and the introduction to the joys
> of the body and of camaraderie and of trust.
>
> —*From Pixote, with Love*, Jacson Ribeiro

Distributor cap. That was it. Pretty simple to fix. Tony owned a mechanic shop now. Had for the last fifteen years. They sat in the cluttered, grease-bespattered, dusty office and drank instant coffee, and reminisced in that way only fellow time-voyagers can do, having commenced on their journey at the same instant in history, feeling the same tick and the same tock. Remember that time Ms. Graham found that cockroach in her pocketbook and peed herself right there in class? Remember Greg Thomas and that time he fell out of the second-story window? That fool. Where is he now? You heard about Tammy Johnson. Mrs. Edgar, the math teacher. Yeah, a wreck, about five years ago . . . The very stuff of pop tunes, the currency of middle age and growing older, yet a balm to the creeping sense of grayness, the shared palimpsest of mutual cell death.

"So I been hearing all about you, man. Doing good. Seen pictures of that building you built over in . . . where was it? Saudi Arabia?"

"Dubai, actually."

Tony laughed, and Cicero was amazed at how much his guffaw sounded like the young jock he knew, had known. "*Shiiiit.* Du-fucking-bai. That's all right, man." He raised his hand for a high-five. "Hey, this coffee is worse than dog piss. Want something stronger?"

"Well, you know I was planning to drive all the way back tonight . . ."

Tony didn't heed Cicero's halfhearted objection, and retrieved from a file cabinet an unopened bottle of Canadian Mist whiskey. He took down two dusty plastic cups from over his desk and gave a boyish wink as he poured them both two fingers each. "Come on, motherfucker, drink up. I'm enjoying myself now. I know you can handle your liquor, fancy-pants. If you want, you can crash at my place and leave early in the morning."

One drink led to five. The clock on the wall read 12:03. Histories had been recounted, but more of the distant past had been reheated than the recent vintage. Tony's marriage ("Yeah, I married Toni Wofford. Yeah, I know. Too damn cute for words. 'Tony and Toni.' I got sick of that shit by the end of the first week"). Tony's children ("Can you believe I've got a girl who's graduated college, one who's a freshman at State, and another who's going to Spelman in the fall? Who's the old fucker now?"). Tony's divorce ("Just got bored, man. That's the onliest way I can put it. Make sense of it").

After one of those pauses, the seventh of the seven-minute lulls that attend all conversations, Tony said: "Sorry to hear about your man. That was rough. Tisha Ann said you were real broke up about it and all. My condolences."

For the first time that evening Cicero was confronted by the fact that he had not spoken much at all about his life; that he had not acknowledged the fact of his queerdom and of his life with a rather famous gay man.

"Thanks, man." They raised their plastic cups to Jacson, who, Cicero thought, in an oblique way, was responsible for this reunion.

> It was Bianca Jagger who said to me, at a party in London for the Crown Prince of Sweden: "People don't care if you're gay, darling. They only care if you know which designer is in this year."
>
> —*From Pixote, with Love*, Jacson Ribeiro

"He won't go, Cicero."

Tisha Ann had been the rock of the family. Cicero had watched her go from tomboy to small-town beauty queen to wife of a local used car dealer to mother of three. From scrawny girl-child to matriarch. He marveled and trembled a little. Time was not a wingèd chariot. It was a space shuttle. A battlestar. A comet.

"I just spoke with him yesterday, Tish. I mean, how long can he keep this up? I've already sent in the check. They're expecting him next week."

"You tell him that then."

"I did."

The true guilt he felt was when he heard the sorrow in his cousin's voice. She seemed to manifest her concern more palpably, more achingly than he could approach. When he spoke with her—she who had been on hand to watch her father's health decline, to watch the diabetes ravage his once-strong body, to see him wheelchair-bound—Cicero somehow wanted to tap into that sense of empathy, that feeling of betrayal, to be able to put himself in his uncle's place and understand the outrage of what they were asking. But Cicero was an engineer, he thought in terms of quantities and spatial relationships and mathematical solutions—or that's the excuse he gave himself.

"You're going to have to come down here, man. I just can't. I can't do it. I'm sorry."

Jacson had been dead for only a few months. Cicero was dwelling—not really living—in too much house on the North Shore of Maryland. An easy daily drive into the DC office. He did not want to go make his uncle move. He wanted to tell her to instruct her fat husband to do it, but Roger was afraid of Dax, had been even before he married Tisha Ann. That trip was the first time Cicero took Jacson's behemoth instead of his trusty Honda. At least he'd be comfortable in driving to his discomfort.

Cicero had expected pyrotechnics, yelling and screaming, demonic ravings, curses, disownment—he'd actually asked the Reverend Lazarus Barden to stop by in the event that his uncle became totally unhinged. But Dax Cross said not a mumbling word, though his eyes communicated poxes and hexes that should have turned his nephew into stone. This Korean War veteran, this high school social studies teacher, this vice-principal, this single parent of two, this trustee of the First Baptist Church, this man who had taken in his late sister's boy as his own—now one-legged from diabetes and rolled out of the only home he'd ever known, ancestral, fruit tree-surrounded, lushly carried-for and tended and mended over the years; now ushered into the anteroom of the great undiscovered country. Not so great.

The greeting at the nursing home was pro forma, and as they went through the motions, it felt to Cicero as if he'd done this before, seen it done before. Dull industrial carpet. Functional-though-boring furniture of wood and cheap chrome and stain-resistant upholstery. On the freshly painted serge-brown walls: framed posters of kittens and puppy dogs and baby pigs, biblical quotations, positive affirmations from long-dead gurus of life. The administrator, the wife of a cousin, coiffured and dressed as if she were going to a nightclub, almost rushed through her instructions, her reassurances, and all the while his uncle remained stone. Crossed his arms. A sphinx. They tucked him in bed, the orderly having lifted the once 250-pound gentleman farmer and football coach like a sack of flour.

"Okay, Dax. I'll call you when I get home. See if the number works."

"Go to hell." The first and last thing Dax had said to him the day they moved Dax into assisted living.

THAT NIGHT in Tony's house on Tony's couch—a rather large and comfortable couch—Cicero tossed about, not able to sleep. His mind sizzling with this last visit with his uncle; with his past and upcoming meeting with Justin Harbinson; with Tisha Ann; with the damn Lexus; with the prospect of the firm offer for his family's farmland from local land baron Percy Terrell and his Terrell Corporation (Dax's land abutted a new housing development Percy's family was building); with the abiding grief over dead Jacson that felt like background radiation with the half-life of uranium-238, not going anywhere anytime soon; with Tony and the memory of Tony. Tony then and now.

That hug. Just before bed. Very tight. Lingering a bit too long. Two middle-aged men with more than a few unnecessary bulges poking out on their once-sleek bodies. Alone together in the wee quiet of the morning. A brushing of lips against the side of the cheek. Just my imagination? The song, annoying as hell, by the Temptations kept playing over again, over again, over again in his mind: "It was just my imagination / Running away with me."

He had known Tony since kindergarten. He had been like the buildings of his childhood—just there. They were tight friends that year. Rarely spoke the next. He saw Tony here and there, at church, at vacation Bible school, on field trips. They traded comic books. They played basketball sometimes.

Sometimes they'd sit together in the school cafeteria and trade in the latest innocuous gossip about who was zooming whom, about TV shows, about Carolina versus State basketball.

The thought that truly bothered Cicero: Was I picking up some true sexual tension between us, back in the truck, between sips of whiskey, on the drive back home, in the hug? Or was it just . . . ?

He had not thought about Tony in over a decade. When he visited home, he spent most of his time with his family. Tony was not a churchgoer. His name had simply not come up in conversation. Just once. Only once. One of those dread, hormone-filled, adolescent, penis-driven, oh-so-happy happenstances. Their junior year in high school. Cicero's only claim to athletic fame was running. He ran the mile. Tony did the fifty-yard dash. That day at a track meet in Wilmington at Hoggard High School, they had both set school records. Cicero hitched a ride with Tony back home. Was it the spring air? The azaleas and the pollen and the fragrance of fresh-cut grass? The high of success? The mutual intoxication of sweat and naked thighs? The unstoppable sense of maleness? Unstoppable maleness? Tony's hand between his legs, his between Tony's, both taboo and Christmas, and that look and that question: *You wanna stop for a while?* The act had not lasted long—twitches and tingles and pulses and involuntary spasms, a gasp, a sigh—and yet it felt like time inside a beloved song with no grace note at the end, which lingers and lingers on, which continues to vibrate well after the orgasm, well after the panting is done . . .

Cicero continued to fret, and noticed that the sun was

about to rise, and in his fretting—should I go into his room? No, this could be a huge mistake—in his indecision and confusion and remembrance of things adolescent, he realized not only that he had forgotten all the burdens of the last few months, but that he was feeling teetotatiously alive, that he was sensing afresh an old stirring he'd somehow bid adieu with Jacson's death, even before Jacson had gone.

The Temptations kept on playing in his mind, and he did not mind at all. He loved the Temptations.

> When my doctor told me the dread news, I said:
> "I must simply live faster."
>
> —*From Pixote, with Love*, Jacson Ribeiro

"I don't know, Mr. Cross. I'm not . . . well . . . let's see if I can express what I'm feeling when I see it . . . I'm wondering, you see . . . if . . ."

Jacson was right. Justin Harbinson did look exceptionally cute when he was spouting bullshit. Somehow Cicero had talked the young gazillionaire into going through with the construction of his monument, at the tender age of thirty-seven. Perhaps the death of Jacson made JH value the project even more than his doubts over the design: Jacson had created for his tomb an adobe shack, built from real adobe bricks imported from Mexico. Cherry trees and cedars and lotuses afloat in storybook ponds. Footbridges over trickling streams. Pattern-raked pebbles, whose contours bespoke Kamakura peace and warlords long dead and Prince Buddha's promise. Tranquil? Yes. But Zen? Just expensive.

"I mean I'm feeling . . . Aztec, you know. Some deep Tenoch-titlan roots. I really dig that. I mean, like *wow!* But, Mr. Cross, and I'm saying this with respect. I don't mean to sound shallow. And I know how intensely spiritual and intelligent and . . . well, *spiritual*, Mr. Ribeiro was. But, Mr. Cross. Golly gee. Well. Does it work? I mean, with the rest of the place, I mean."

It didn't take an editor at *Architectural Digest* to see what was making Harbinson so uncomfortable. And for a moment Cicero felt bad for Justin Harbinson, knowing full well that, by and by, the kid would get over his reverence for the dead and over the fear of his own death, and tear down the joke built at his expense. Maybe he'd realize that a dead man had used him for his final chuckle. Or maybe he would not. In either case, Cicero no longer found it funny.

"Mr. Harbinson. New construction—seeing it for the first time—can be shocking. You should live with it for a time, before making any rash decisions."

Harbinson stood still and gazed at Cicero as if trying to figure out this idea of "living with something." As if wondering how much time one let pass before enough living was done. As if wondering if this was his way out, if he could erase this many-hundred-thousand-dollar mistake from his life like next year's tax write-off.

"You should know that the steel beams you see"—Cicero pointed out the chamber that held the ancient bricks in place like an ornate cage, its design clearly inspired by the Napoleon III period of Mexican colonialism—"the material will, over time, oxidize in an amazing way. The color will deepen, and the orange steel will turn a moody, deep, rich purple. I'm not sure if I made that clear."

"Of course, Mr. Cross. Thank you for reminding me." JH paused and blinked at the eyesore, trying not to grimace, and failing. "You know, on paper it looked . . . well, better."

Cicero sighed, and turned to leave. "No, Mr. Harbinson. Actually, on paper it looked much worse."

As FAR AS Cicero was concerned, hospice care workers were angels walking upon the earth. His admiration for them would never dim.

Jacson's death, like all his life, had been something of a production. The house in Maryland had not long been finished when he had become bedridden. Visitors were legion, making the trek to Chesapeake Bay to pay their respects. Disco music and reggae and bossa nova ("Too much bossa nova, you think? It is sad. Give me happy, no? Play me some Motown, baby, gimme the Four Tops, no?") resounded throughout the house on the state-of-the-art sound system.

Ten tumultuous years. It had not been bliss, but mostly happy, usually fun, always interesting. He had known Jacson was seropositive the first night he climbed into bed with him. It never once occurred to Cicero not to take the Brazilian giant into his arms, into his heart. His funny valentine. The house on the Maryland shore had been like their child, two redoubtable architects conceiving it together, from the ground up. Nine years in the making. Insanely large. Insanely eclectic. Bordering on bad taste—Leonardo's Florence meets Ramses' Memphis meets the huts of Congo and the temples of Indonesia—but they pulled it off. And damn near went broke doing it. That Casa Malandragem would win awards was a foregone conclusion. "I shall die here," Jacson had said on the night they spent on the bare land after they had purchased it, frisky amid the brush and weeds and bugs and dirt. That was the last time Cicero had allowed himself to sob. But they were actually tears of joy. Men compromised with HIV were living for decades now, the presaged death actually felt as far away to him as did his own.

Jacson died after lunch, one overcast May day—when war was imminent and big, wide America, as a lot, had largely forgotten about acquired immunodeficiency syndrome—while taking a nap on the deck overlooking Chesapeake Bay, after having a lightly spicy gazpacho and a few saltine crackers. As much as he could hold down by that time.

He had, of course, written out his funeral to the last detail: Washington National Cathedral. Harlem Boys Choir. Jessye Norman. A memorial capoeira dance. For Cicero the most disquieting moment was back at the house, with Jacson's adoptive parents, now in their seventies, simply bewildered, unprepared. "He was the strongest man I ever met," Professor Mauskoff had said.

> Cicero and I slept naked that night, on a blanket under the stars. We made love on the land where we would build Casa Malandragem. I knew I would die there. I cannot tell you what peace that knowledge gave me. We will all die, one fine day. To know the place, at least, is more than most can hope for.
>
> —*From Pixote, with Love,* Jacson Ribeiro

He awoke to the smell of eggs and bacon and coffee (the real kind this time) and toast and grits. Lovely grits. Precious grits. How sweet the taste.

Shirtless, Tony's beefy brown brawn was no less alluring than his teenage centaur-like tawny form. And he could cook too. Damn.

"Hope you ain't pissed that I hijacked you last night. Was just happy to see you, bro."

For a while they munched and spoke of random things, nothing like the intense rehashing of history undergone the night before. This was light. This was denouement.

Finally: "You take many meds?"

"Meds?"

"You know. For—"

Cicero had never been what is commonly known as a morning person. He hated to think at this hour, but Tony's meaning became clear.

"Oh. Oh. No. No, I'm not. I don't have. I'm negative. We didn't. We weren't. I'm clean."

Tony did not look at him. "I had just assumed. Sorry."

"Nothing to be sorry about, man. It's all good."

Tony sopped up the last of his grits with the last remnants of his toast. He chewed. "Yeah," he said. "Seven years for me."

Cicero just stared at him, coffee cup suspended—at a ridiculous angle, he would later think back to himself as he replayed and replayed and replayed this moment in his mind's eye, seeing himself seeing his old buddy as if for the first time, that morning, in the April-bright North Carolina light that streamed through the lemon curtains like a children's drink. "Oh."

Oh and oh and oh and oh. The coffee was now lukewarm.

"Damn, man. I'm sorry," Cicero finally managed to squeeze out. His toes. They felt numb all of a sudden.

"You remember Mr. Thompson?" Tony was looking at him now, and smiling, with that same sweet, uncomplicated openness he had had yesterday inside the truck.

"The algebra teacher? Track coach? Yeah, I remember him."

"'Member what he used to say all the time. His fucking mantra?"

Without pausing they both said: "*It is what it is.*"

The unison of their laughter rang out like an out-of-tune donkey chorus for quite a few minutes. Exactly the sort of laughter that chases away evil spirits and awkward moments and haunted dreams.

"Ain't thought about that ole coot in a coon's age." Tony got up to collect the dishes.

"You look good. No problems?"

"Ah, no, man, I ain't been sick since I tested positive. Haven't even had a cold or nothing. This new stuff they got . . . lotta fucking pills, but man, it's something else. Not like . . ."

"Yeah, I feel ya."

Before breakfast he had imagined his leave-taking to have been a raucous thing, a backslapping, I'll-call-you-when-I'm-in-town-next-and-we'll-really-hang parting, half meant, half expected. But now his parting was a heavy thing, a molten thing, a thing that drug down on him like the shackles of both their ancestors. He did not hesitate to kiss Tony full on the lips, and Tony responded as if with relief. Such big warm lush delicious lips they were. Tony grabbed his butt as they kissed.

Cicero didn't say he'd call. He knew at this point words were like JH's, only what happened next mattered. He meant good. It wasn't enough to say you'd come back. Coming back was coming back.

Cicero sat in his goddamn fucking expensive shitty luxury car, his dead lover's fucking expensive shitty Lexus, and thought: *I can't leave stuff like this.* He lost track of time as he sat. He looked out over the cornfields, the green so young, so struggling to take to the sky. Immature things, but too big for crows to pluck. For the engineer the solution finally presented itself, the same way quadratic equations, all at once, materialized before his inner eye. The simplicity. The rightness. What is land? What is a building? What does a man really own? He started the car, and drove back. Back to Seraphim Care Assisted Living.

HE SAT for a long time. In the chair that was a knockoff of a knockoff of a knockoff of a once-fresh design by Le Corbusier. Like the images on Plato's Cave. Uncle Dax had taught him all about Plato. He had made him read the *Republic* when he was twelve, and made him write a report on it.

Dax Cross lay on his bed, flicking through *Time* magazine as if it had offended him, glancing up at C-SPAN every few minutes, playing on the television bolted to the ceiling, hanging there like laboratory equipment waiting to be fired up. Dax ignored his nephew with admirable convincingness. After about thirty minutes of the silent treatment, Cicero said: "Okay, Uncle Dax. We won't sell the place. I'll sell the house in Maryland. Use that to pay . . . well. We'll keep the land in the family."

Dax spoke up quickly, as if they'd been chatting for the last half an hour. "Don't do me no favors."

"I thought that's what you wanted?"

"It is what I wanted. But I want you to understand, you knucklehead. I want you to get it. So you go ahead and do what you got to do. I'm done with your black faggoty ass. I ain't going to forgive you. I am not pleased with you."

Cicero winced. "Don't you get tired of this hate? This bitterness? I mean, can't you see I'm just trying to do the right thing?"

Dax flipped through the magazine some more. He looked again up at the Senate hearing. Cicero wondered if he even knew who was being confirmed. "Fuck off."

Cicero turned to go. As he got to the door he heard his uncle say:

"Right thing to do anyway."

Cicero wheeled around, but Dax was not looking at him. He had the magazine over his face. And he had turned the television off.

The Eternal Glory That Is Ham Hocks

Every man has his price.

—Howard R. Hughes Jr.

My mother did not tell me about Howard Hughes's visit to Tims Creek on her deathbed; she had first mentioned that curious bit of family history several years before, while we shucked and cleaned ears of sweet corn, fresh from the fields, each kernel pearl-white and sweet like candy.

"Who?" I had said, absently, thinking I had misheard her, focusing instead on how good it was going to be to boil these ears up, a bit of salt, a knob of butter—you simply couldn't get corn like this in LA.

The radio had been playing and at the top of the news had been a report about another settlement in the ongoing battle over the will of the late great reclusive multigazillionaire. "Who's that?" I repeated.

"Howard Hughes," Mama said. "Came and asked me to come work for him."

I didn't drop the corn, exactly, for I believed I had misheard, misunderstood, misapprehended my mother, but I did squeeze it a tad overmuch, regrettably causing an unsightly bruise.

"What do you mean 'Howard Hughes wanted you to work for him'?" She had my attention now.

"Oh, it was a long time ago. We were living back at the other place. In Mama's house. Your daddy was stationed in the Philippines. Your sister was just a little bitty thing."

"Mama?"

"Yes, baby."

"What are you talking about?"

She gave me that look that only a woman who had taught elementary school for decades can muster.

"Howard Hughes wanted me to come work for him."

There is a moment when someone you've known all your born days, someone you respect beyond reason, with the force of superstition; there is a moment when that person says something so incredible it forces you to recalibrate, rejigger, rethink the blueprints of the universe we each haul around in our heads.

Before I could say anything she said: "Oh but that was a long, long time ago. Long, long time. Before you were born."

"Why didn't you . . . What? When? Mama, you're joking."

"No." She picked up another ear of corn. "Mr. Thompson sure grew some pretty corn this year, didn't he?"

"Mama?"

"What?"

"What did Howard Hughes . . ." I paused, not certain if I wanted to know the answer to the question I was about to ask. "What did Howard Hughes want you to do for him?"

She laughed, that laugh I now miss so much: girlish, eyes closed, involving the shoulders, not quite coquettish but somehow apology and delight at the same time.

"He wanted me to come cook for him. Can you believe that? The richest man in the world. Shoot."

My abandonment of high finance for food was not gradual. In fact it came to me in a dream, very Old Testament prophet-like. Alone in my bed in my Riverside Drive apartment, I smelled a powerful aroma, so powerful from my childhood (neurologists say that smell hallucinations are a telltale sign of schizophrenia, but I was well past the age of a psychotic break; past the average age, at least). In my dream I arose and walked to the kitchen, and there on the butcher's block (I didn't actually own a butcher's block at the time, but it seemed right that I would, in this olfactory dream of mine), the sumptuous spread glistened and steamed, foods from my North Carolina boyhood undreamt of on the Upper West Side. Chitlins. Pig feet. Sweetbreads. Chicken feet. Gizzards and livers and head cheese. There were sweet potatoes and tomatoes and collard greens and okra and squash and, yes, sweet corn. Before long in walked a woman, naked, save for one of those pirate hats with the great plumes, jutting up and out and over, vividly red it was and full and large, which, altogether, is undeniably sexy, and which, for this narrative, would be a digression—needless to say when I awoke it was the aromas, the sights, the warm feelings of the food that lingered with me most.

I waited for a decent hour before I called my mother.

"Can you tell me how you cook your chicken livers?"

"Baby, why are you cooking chicken livers at six thirty in the morning? I thought you just had a bagel and coffee for breakfast."

"I know, Ma, I know. I just had a craving. Now, come on, talk me through it."

Thus began what my bosses called a slow descent, but my future teachers called an upward spiral. I can mark the day, practically the hour. Thereafter I would call home almost daily, often before shopping and while cooking, to pick my mother's brain and to get her advice. I would go home more frequently to watch her in action, to see how she washed the greens, to see what she put in the water with her hog mawls, to learn her seasonings, her timing, her heat. I was learning a new definition of love.

BETWEEN MY dad's love of history and my mom's love of learning in general and her wide reading, it's not hard to figure out how I'd chosen law. Applying law to investment banking was not quite so obvious, but after five years I knew the world of bonds and stocks and mergers and acquisitions was not going to be for me.

When I told Mama I was quitting Drexel and had been admitted to a topflight culinary school in Vermont, her sigh of apparent relief made me smile and made me feel a quantity of relief myself.

※

ALLENE GANO HUGHES died during childbirth. She was thirty-nine years old. Her only son, Howard, was away at a high-toned California prep school at the time. The separation had been difficult, initially, between mother and son, for they had a strange, some would say unnaturally close, relationship. They shared a mania for cleaning and a barely kept-in-check hypochondria. The call to inform his son of his mother's death was probably the most difficult thing Howard Robard Hughes Sr. had ever had to do in his life.

By all accounts, though not a particularly good man, a man who found it difficult to keep his penis in his pants when it came to other women, a man who preferred to be away from home most of the time, he felt a love for his wife and child that was, nonetheless, genuine. He was good at the love part. And he was even better at business.

Originally a wildcat Texas oilman of middling accomplishments, Daddy Hughes one day realized there might be some serious cash money in building a better drill bit. What he dreamed up became a dream for the oil business, and his rewards were mighty. By the time of Junior's birth, his father was well on his way to fossil-fuel greatness, with a wife who came from old Texas aristocracy, and who would one day be able to give his son the whole world.

HOWARD SR. built a sprawling brick mansion on Yoakum Boulevard in Houston's well-heeled Southside in 1910. After Allene's funeral, young Howard returned to the Thacher School in California, but Howard Sr. wanted his son back in Houston with him. The father argued with the school's headmaster, who thought being away, with boys his own age, learning, would be far better for the boy than to be at home with an overindulgent father. But after a year Howard R. Hughes Sr. got his way and his seventeen-year-old son returned to his side at the massive house on Yoakum Boulevard, where young Howard would meet a young woman, age thirty at the time, a woman hired not long after his mother's death, to cook and clean for the tiny family.

Inez Cross. Later Inez Cross Pickett. My grandmother.

MY MOTHER never got to see my restaurant in California. I think she would have appreciated it. I cooked for her, during those last years, showed her what the LA papers had dubbed Nouvelle Soul Cuisine without my prompting or blessing but with little objection. Her favorite was my candied yams. She did not approve of my collard greens. And though she found my Frenchified calf's livers admirable, my version of her chicken livers she found incomprehensible.

I could tell she was trying not to hurt my feelings.

"Hmmmmm," she said, "how much do you charge for this one?"

When I told her she asked, "And you sell a lot of them, do you?"

"Yes, ma'am, a good many."

"Hmmmmm, now these chitlins are so creamy. So good."

IN 1966 there was only one motel in Crosstown, which was the closest lodging in proximity to the wee village of Tims Creek.

Completed just the year before, the Crosstown Inn and Motor Lodge was modest by almost any standard, all painted cinder block and particleboard and veneer and an unfortunate nautical theme that had yet to be consigned to the dustbin of interior decorating; only fourteen units, seven equipped with two twin beds, and seven with a double each; the diner, busiest in the morning with its fried egg and ham special, was where the owner, John Bradham, earned his mortgage. The rooms were mostly used by the rare out-of-towner there to see someone in the county jail or by families en route to the beaches, another fifty miles east.

Which is why, when the two tall men in black suits arrived, driving their brand-new and shiny black Lincoln with the California license plates, and snooped around, looking in places your average, run-of-the-mill motel-overnighter never looks—it more than puzzled John Bradham. But that puzzlement would be surpassed when, bright and early, the tall blond-headed fellow came to the front desk and informed Mr. Bradham of the desire on the part of a certain unknown "employer" to purchase the place, lock, stock, and diner. The monetary figure that the blond-headed man in the black suit offered was four times what Bradham had owed to the First Mercantile Savings and Loan, and yet, so dumbfounded, so incredulous, so perplexed was Mr. Bradham that he—after managing to pick his bottom lip up from the floor—simply said: "Well, I'm just going to have to think on that. Can you let me tell you tomorrow?"

The young blond-headed man—himself a poor shopkeeper's son from a small town in northern Utah, who found this verdant, humid East Coast hamlet peculiar to say the least, beheld the small-town businessman with something resembling awe. And even admiration. Who could say no to that kind of money?

That is exactly what Noah Dietrich had asked over the telephone line, when the young man made his report. Dietrich said that along with a set of choice words which offended the young Mormon's pristine sensibilities. Dietrich was the man who ran Howard Hughes's far-flung empire, and who some believe was responsible for making him a billionaire.

"Who does that little hillbilly think he is?" (Yes, Dietrich called John Bradham a hillbilly, which, for the record, demonstrates a deficiency in geographic knowledge on Dietrich's part—York County is in the Coastal Plain, and there are no hills there.)

Dietrich was a busy man at the moment, even busier than usual. He had just presided over the forced sale of his employer's stake in Trans World Airlines, TWA, which had netted the Texan over half a billion dollars. And now Dietrich's boss had moved to Las Vegas and was buying casino after casino after casino. Even more aggravating was the little fact that the mysterious heir had locked himself up in a suite at the Dunes and was only seeing his Mormon bodyguards; not even his wife was allowed to see him.

Dietrich was busy. Dietrich was preoccupied. Dietrich was mystified. Dietrich had his hands full. And now Howard Hughes wanted to go to Bumfuck, North Carolina? Jesus H. Christ on a tricycle!

Every motherfucker has a price, the Boss always liked to say.

When Noah Dietrich told the young blond-headed man in the black suit and impressively narrow black tie to go back to John Bradham, that very minute, and when he told the upright Mormon how much to offer the thrifty Scots-Irish businessman, it literally made the Latter-Day Saint commence to sweat. He was sweating when he presented the offer; he was sweating when Bradham said: "If you want it that bad, just show me the moolah and you can have my wife too for that kinda money. Hell, take my daughter too. Hot dog I reckon! And by the way, who do you work for again?"

"I'm sorry, sir, but my employer wishes to remain anonymous."

This is how Howard Robard Hughes Jr. kept his visit to Tims Creek, North Carolina, in the fall of 1966, a secret. For, after having set a very well-paid private investigator on the trail of one Negress, named Inez Pickett (née Cross), and after she was located, and after he sent an agent to purchase the pissant motel to be prepared for his brief visit—this sum, by the way, for Hughes, who was, at the time, pulling down roughly $50 to $60 million per annum, was far less than what he offhandedly gave for a single secondhand jet—and after a team of workers drove up from Georgia, directly from the Lockheed plants with whom he had a long-standing and oh-so-lucrative relationship; and after they modified a few rooms to be acceptable to the Boss's strict parameters—all of this happened within the course of a week, seven days—then and only then could he himself helm a DC-3 with his retinue in tow (who, to a man—and they were all men, all Mormons, for the record—really hated it when the employer decided to pilot the plane; he didn't really inspire a great deal of aviatory confidence during those strange and stranger days). Thus a week after hatching the notion to find Inez Cross did he—shaven, pressed, fresh-looking, and ever so charming—show up at the door of my mother.

Her mother, Inez Cross Pickett, had died in 1963.

AFTER HIS mother's death, young Howard was never quite comfortable in the Yoakum Boulevard mansion. Not only was he haunted by memories of his mother, but also by memories of a simpler, freer and less complicated time, and of his mechanical explorations: like the time his dad allowed him to purchase a brand-new car, and to take it completely apart and put it back together again.

The courses he was taking at the Rice Institute were fun enough, but nothing seemed to scratch this itch he had. He didn't even know where to scratch.

The house only had a bare-bones staff. Despite Senior's desire to get his son back home, he still traveled extensively, leaving his son alone in the many-roomed house with his many man-sized toys and many-footed staff. Teenage Howard was not the sort to befriend the help.

The problem arose when Inez did the cooking.

"What the hell is this?"

"I'm sorry?" Inez had said, coming out of the kitchen into the dining room with the imposing table where sat the frowning scion.

"What is this?"

"It's fried chicken, Mr. Hughes." She was by all accounts a tall woman, thin, yet sturdy, sure of herself, with a farmer's daughter's droll humor.

"No. No. No. That! What is that!"

Inez had been left to her own devices when it came to the meals and shopping. When she was first hired, Annette, Allene Hughes's sister, Howard's aunt, set her up and familiarized her with the place. HRH Sr. was a steak-and-potatoes man. In fact he resented overly fancy food, the sort favored by his late wife and her ilk. Despite his desire to be counted among their number, he still thought of himself, at root, as a wildcatter, a man among men. A Texan. A beef-eater.

Taking her cue from the father, Inez kept the meals simple, and in the process reverted to her Down East North Carolina ways.

"What is it?" He was pointing toward a mound of lime-green beans awash in a thin, creamy sauce with flecks of red meat afloat amid the legumes.

"Butter beans. They were on sale and—"

"On sale? . . . Butter. Beans. Well . . . okay. I see . . ." He poked the beans with his fork, as if they were somehow alien. He sampled them as if they were rumored to do some magical thing like cure heartbreak. After a few quizzical chews and a swallow he proclaimed: "Not bad. Not bad at all."

"Thank you, sir."

"And is this ham? You put *ham* in the beans? And butter too? I don't quite understand . . ."

"That's ham hock, sir. You put ham hocks in the vegetables to season 'em up good. No butter. Just ham hocks."

"Fascinating," Howard said, and went back to studying an engine diagram while eating absentmindedly as always, completely forgetting about my grandmother.

How MY grandmother—whom I never met—a young African-American woman born in a teeny NC town in 1892, found herself in Houston, Texas, in the 1920s, I've yet to discover. There are suggestions that she was following a man—a man who did not become my grandfather. Rumors of following a family to Texas to work for them; rumors of a job offer. Ultimately I have no clue as to how much experience she had cooking for the well-to-do, or how good she was at it.

ON JANUARY 14, 1924, Howard Hughes Sr. dropped dead. At nineteen young Howard was thirsting to be his own man, he had no intentions of waiting two years for his legal majority to kick in. Therefore he had his lawyers quickly buy out his relatives' inherited interest in the Hughes Tool Company, to a one, thus making it completely and totally his, and, more important, he convinced a judge to declare him an adult. By June he had married a Houston aristocrat—like his mother— to silence any naysayers about his prematurely acquired mantle of manhood. He moved to Hollywood, and later that same year he hired Noah Dietrich. The house on Yoakum Boulevard was closed up, the staff let go. Junior never said goodbye to Inez Cross. A lawyer handed her her final check.

ACCORDING TO my mother, my sister found a particular fascination with Howard Hughes's shoes. Odd, when you figure she would one day become a buyer for Nordstrom. Hughes was sixty-one and unaccustomed to dealing with anyone who didn't work for him and fear him. Three-year-old black girls simply didn't figure into his cosmology.

"I'm really sorry to hear about your loss, ma'am. She was a fine lady. Nineteen sixty-three, did you say?"

"Yes, sir. She died just after Christmas."

Hughes remained silent and the silence grew long and uneasy.

"Can I get you something, Mr. . . . I'm sorry. What was your name again?"

"Hughes, ma'am, Howard Hughes. I'm a Junior. Your mother, she worked for my father. And me."

"I see, Mr. Hughes. Let me get you some ice tea—Veronica! Leave that man's shoelaces alone! Come here—I'm so sorry, Mr. Hughes."

That done, sweaty glass of ice tea in his hand, the awkward silence returned.

"So, Mr. Hughes, is there anything I can do for you?"

Hughes put down his glass. "Mrs. Cross . . . I mean Pickett—"

"Actually, I'm a Chasten now. My husband he's stationed in the Philippines at the moment. He's a mechanic in the army."

Hughes's eyes lit up at the word "mechanic," but a harsh, single-minded, pragmatic look took over his brow: "Do you cook, ma'am?"

"Of course I do, but—"

"Now, see here. I'll get right to the point, Mrs. Chasten. I'm not a man to dilly and dally around if you get my meaning.

"See, your mama she used to cook for me, see. Right after my dear mama passed. And, well, I'll tell you, Mrs. Chasten, that was about the most—how do I put it?— the most memorable food I've had in all my born days. Unusual. Satisfying. Like nothing I'd had before, or, to be honest, since. Now, I'm not the sort of man who spends a lot of time thinking about food, myself. Take after my paw like that. But your mama's cooking . . . well . . ." Howard Hughes stood up, as if the need to pace had overcome him, but when his head came so close to the ceiling, he seemed to think better of it, and sat back down, but now perching on the edge of the seat, his large frame casting a shadow upon the room.

"To be completely honest, I didn't really appreciate it so good while she was there, but after she left it kinda lingered, if you get my meaning. Never had a biscuit quite like hers, you see. In fact, I think I can honestly say hers was the first biscuit to cross these lips. You see. Recently here I've been hankering, if that's exactly the word I want, hankering for her cuisine something fierce."

It took my mother a while to receive and digest what the industrialist—who to her, at the moment, was just some tall white fellow, a little strange, who clearly, in his better days, had enjoyed charm and good looks, but who now was riding on the steam of his money, and who obviously had more of that commodity than he had any clue what to do with. "Well," Mama said, "I'm sure she would have been proud and happy to know you liked her cooking so, mister. Proud and happy."

"Mrs. Chasten, I would like for you to come back with me. Back to Nevada, where I've recently taken up residence, and cook for me. The food your mama used to cook."

My mom laughed. She always laughed when she got nervous. Cook? Nevada? Me? This was simply too too much.

"Don't worry, I'll make it worth your while. Yessiree Bob." Hughes then called out a sum that made my mother stop laughing.

"Excuse me," she said, "you can't be serious."

Hughes doubled the figure, with a casual, imperious air, meant to indicate how little money meant to him, but oddly enough it had exactly the opposite effect.

My mother rose to her feet. "I'm sorry, sir. But I'm going to have to decline your offer. But I thank you."

Hughes, undeterred, pronounced a figure that even now, in the twenty-first century, just seems ridiculous, an insult even. Which is exactly how my mother took it. Her eyes narrowed at him.

"Mister. My husband is overseas. I'm a schoolteacher with a three-year-old and another one on the way"—and she put both her hands on her big belly, on me—"Now, I don't know how you folk do things out there in Texas and California and NE-vada, but here in North Carolina, I put my family and my responsibilities first. Above all else. Above money. And frankly I don't know what kind of game you think you're running, but I don't want any part of it, and in fact I suggest it's time you were on your way."

Hughes stood and picked up his hat. "Ma'am," he said, "in my experience everybody has their price."

"You don't have that much money, mister."

At that Howard Robard Hughes Jr. laughed. A big, loud, long, mocking guffaw. He was still chortling as he walked out the door, snickering as he got into the backseat of the Lincoln, chuckling as it drove away down the dirt road and vanished into the ether.

APPARENTLY HUGHES didn't intend on giving up that easily. He sent lawyers several times over the next couple of months with contracts and sometimes with checks, once with a bag of money. Literally. One wonders: Why didn't he just hire another chef? One of the fifteen thousand or so truly excellent cooks working on any given day all over the planet

Earth? But this mania—one among the many he collected and harbored and cultivated like virulent viruses in the petri dish of his soul—wasn't really about food, in the end, it was about time, time lost, time gone, about remembrance, about a feeling. Money can't buy you love, a famous song says—but that's just one of the many several things beyond its grasp.

In truth I can empathize about biscuits and my kins-women. One of my earliest childhood memories: early June, blueberry season. My mother would macerate the plump new berries, briefly, only for a few minutes, with the slight-est touch of sugar. Next, over a fire they'd go, gently heated, a slight simmer, creating the simplest of simple sugars, but somehow beatified, blessed and blessedly blue.

When sopped up with one of those steam-white and steam-light biscuits created with cold butter just before the first rooster awoke, the resultant reaction in-mouth arrested the tongue and captured the brain.

For a boy with no knowledge of sex, this basic sensual experience, firing off every nerve ending with sunshine and delight, taught me everything I would need to know about orgasms long before I ever had need for the word.

All Howard Hughes's real estate holdings were owned by the Summa Corporation, which, years after his will was settled, was finally sold to the Rouse Company. When I last checked, they still owned the Crosstown Inn and Motor Lodge, and the place hasn't changed much. The eggs are still greasy, the ham tough as shoe leather, the coffee fit for removing toilet clogs.

———

Daddy did well as an electrician, very well indeed, over the years. And Mama got her master's degree—it took many years of driving back and forth to East Carolina University twice a week. She became a principal of the local elementary school, and for a few years before she retired, she was a county school supervisor.

When I asked her why she turned Hughes down, she said, merely, "I didn't like the smug way he asked. Like he could buy and sell folk on a whim. Besides, if he was going to pay somebody that kind of money—which I simply, simply couldn't begin to believe—for somebody to stir him up some shrimp and grits—I know he had to be stone-crazy."

And when I asked why she had never talked about this rare encounter before, she said: "I didn't want your daddy to know, to be frank about it. Do you have any idea what that man would have done if he knew I'd turned down that kind of money?"

Ain't
No Sunshine

While sitting in the sheriff's office, less than an hour after whipping J. C. Stokes with his belt in the parking lot of the IGA food store at Possum Crossing, Pastor Lazarus Barden II remembered exchanging cross words with his aunt Hortensia Barden Parker Compton. He was trying to remember if he had ever spoken that sharply to her before in all his forty-nine years, and if he would ever have to again. The notion did not settle well in his stomach. He reached for his package of Tums.

"I HEAR the Williams place is up for sale," is how she commenced in on the topic. For the last three months, at least, one of their five weekly conversations zeroed in on the matter of his future. Her late brother, his father, had all the delicacy of a damaged bull when discussing personal matters. Aunt Tensy presumed herself a better dancer when it came to such subjects, but her attempts, ultimately, were no less bovine.

"You need to start looking for a place, Lazarus. You can't waste time, baby. I always admired what Miss Maggie did with that place of hers. I figure you give your house to that little witch. Just let her have it. I imagine you can get a good—"

"Aunt Tensy. I have no intention to move."

"Lazarus. Lazarus. Lazarus. Pig foot. You need to wake up and smell the cappuccino, honey. I mean, I don't believe in getting in other people's business. Lord knows I don't. That's always thankless. Lord knows. But son, you need to get this behind you. I know it's not easy, but—"

"Aunt Tensy, you don't know what you're talking about."

"I don't know. I don't . . . Oh, child, please. Everybody in the county knows about it. How long are you going to—"

"I've gotta go now, Aunt Tensy. Gonna be late."

"Fine. Fine. When you're ready, we'll talk."

"No, Aunt Tensy. We're not going to talk. I never want you to bring this up again. Do you hear me? Never. Ever. Again."

When intense, his aunt spoke very quickly: "Boy, I never took you for a fool. I thought you had more sense. I mean you made a mistake marrying that heifer. But we all make mistakes. Lord knows I've made my share. But I did tell you then, to your face. She's no-account. She's trifling. She just wants you for your money. I know that's unkind, but sometimes people need to tell the truth. But you're just like my daddy, and I know sometimes you need—"

"Jesus Christ, woman! I told you I have to go."

For a second—a very rare second—Hortensia was quiet. "I was just trying to help, Lazarus. You don't need to get that kind of tone with me. Boy, I changed your diapers. The least you could do—"

"Yeah, I know. Aunt Tensy always knows better than all these dumb, shit-kicking niggers down here in York County.

Lord knows what we'd do if we didn't have you up in Detroit running our lives. Bye." He flipped his cell phone shut. The only thing he truly loved about a cell phone was the sound of snapping it shut.

Tensy lived in a suburb just outside the Motor City. As far as she was concerned, cellular technology had been invented especially for her. Somehow she obtained more free minutes a day than existed in twenty-four hours, and somehow she managed to use them all. Quiet as it's kept, when Detroit burned in 1968 white people were not the only ones to flee. A legion of black doctors and pharmacists and car salesmen and liquor store owners and the like also absconded to their own Grosse Points and Dearborns. At the time, Hortensia Barden Parker, grown tired of teaching eighth-grade French, received her realtor's license, packed off her youngest son to the Air Force Academy, met some ravenous real estate developers eager to promote sales to the growing black middle class, and she found a way to marry her down-home Southern charm with her social-climbing wishes and her ungainly ambition into becoming a connected real estate broker for well-off Negroes. Now, pushing eighty, the oldest living member of her extended clan, she ran the Barden and Parker families— in her eyes—like the CEO of a corporation. All through his growing up Hortensia would descend upon Tims Creek (now on her second husband, having left the first for a very well-paid GM inspector) in her latest-model white Lincoln— always a Lincoln, always white—in July and in December, rolling out of the driver's seat, ever short and ever widening, showing off her three sons, two short, one tall: one to become a neurosurgeon, one to become an ad executive, one to become an air force colonel; she with her arms full of gifts and stories of accomplishment, and straightaway, before the sun set on the first night, getting into everybody's business. Those childhood memories always conjured a warm feeling, a feeling of awe, a feeling of respect, a feeling of dread.

With the death of his father, nine years before, she noisily asserted her position as the head of the family, presiding over family reunions, giving out shiploads of advice and—like any dictator worth her salt—interest-free loans. No one thought to challenge her right, as the last living child of the Reverend Lazarus Barden, to be the boss of their lives.

AFTER DELIVERING the beating, earlier that morning, at the IGA, in the parking lot, Lazarus Barden II had gotten into his car. He just sat there for a spell, catching his breath—he was hot and sweaty and he felt an alarming tightness not only in his chest but in his belly, and his thighs felt unaccountably sore. His entire shoulder and bicep and forearm burned with an ungodly pain, the sort of pain that directly becomes numbness. His next step did not so much reveal itself to him as a decision as unfold as an inevitability, a preordained edict not to be questioned or examined, just done. Something to head off any further wrongness and wrongheadedness. To be a man, and not an addled, weak, sex-crazed child, like J. C. Stokes. Lazarus Barden II was simply not the sort of person to get into a mess. He was not a messy person.

The drive to Crosstown was only fifteen minutes. The newly plowed fields and farmhouses and filling stations and fields of wildflowers all had a new poignancy about them.

This was azalea time, a riot of color hollering from the hedgerows and front porches and driveways and yard edges even of the most humble dwellings. They shone like a sign. He was not exactly at peace, but he could feel a level of torment with which he had been living—for far too long—now shift into another gear, another place. In some strange way this entire day was very like a song. He was actually moving on. Heretofore he had felt like a tractor stuck in wet clay, now his wheels were finally gaining traction.

The new sheriff's office in Crosstown was a sad new redbrick rectangle, squat and dull and treeless. Just a block away the old courthouse still stood, all blond marble in its smug, Federal Imperial majesty, built when his great-granddaddy was still a slave, no doubt with some of his labor; encircled by two-hundred-year-old pecan trees and even more history. Not even so much as an afterthought, the new sheriff's office and jailhouse did not even rise to the ambition of being forbidding or imposing; just a testament to not caring on so many levels. Only a few years old, the grass had not even taken, offering up bald spots here and there like a beggar's panderings.

Behind the front desk—as high and as long as the bed of a pickup truck—sat his cousin Alfreda in her deputy's uniform.

"Hey, Rus," she said, "what you know good?" Alfreda was a woman who adored hair extensions and arresting colorations. At present her coiffure sported an orangutan-orange, the shade of which Rus Barden didn't find flattering to her. Or to any human being for that matter.

He never figured out if she was a deputy-deputy who actually had a gun or was just a receptionist who wore a deputy's uniform. Moreover she possessed fingernails like daggers, six inches if they were an inch, and encrusted with tiny diamond-like beads, scattered like so many grains of sugar. Watching her work a computer keyboard was akin to witnessing a circus act.

"What brings you to us today?"

"I need to talk with the sheriff, Alfreda. Tony in?"

"No," she said. "He went over to Subway to pick up a sandwich. He should be back tereckly. Pull up a seat and tell me all the good news."

Though he did not feel up to it, he did sit and trade in a little gossip. He had long ago grown weary of small-town gossip, of gloating over the misfortunes, the mistakes, the momentary stupidity of his kinfolk and townfolk and everyday folkfolk. But he was thankful Alfreda was the sort of gossip who brought more than she hauled away. He could let his mind drift as she told him about the latest guess-who-got-arrested-while-wearing-nothing-but-panties stories, while only occasionally chiming in with: "Ain't that something?" or, "What makes folk do stuff like that, I wonder?" As he listened he felt ever more the hypocrite, ever more as if he were getting a foretaste of stories in which he'd star: "Girl, did you hear about the pastor over at Tims Creek? Say he took off his belt and whipped the shit outta that boy who was humping his wife. Uh-huh. Said that nigger came up to him all drunk and told him the next time he calls his house he'd better put his wife on the phone."

Alfreda was soon going to be a very popular woman. The sheriff was taking his time, and after a while the phone began to ring. So Lazarus Barden II sat and waited and wondered.

GINA AND Aunt Tensy had had it out over the phone about six months ago. Rus had not borne witness to the actual conversation, nor did he ever learn the full details of what all had been said, but thereafter when his aunt called and Gina happened to answer the phone she would hand it to him saying either "It's that bitch" or "It's that old bitch from Detroit," loud enough to benefit his father's sister. And his aunt began referring to his wife as a strumpet. In Hortensia Barden Parker Compton's lexicon, a strumpet was about as low as it gets.

Hortensia had never really cottoned to Regina Floyd, and was not shy about her objections to her oldest nephew's marriage. She threatened not to attend the wedding. She threatened to never speak to him again.

He had been thirty-nine, and Gina a fleet twenty-nine. He had never married, she had been divorced for less than a year with a nine-year-old daughter when he began to court and spark her. That phrase had made her laugh. "You so old-fashion," she said. He had known Gina all her life, had witnessed her steps and missteps, had heard all the gossip about her loose ways and dangerous beaus. But that aura worked like catnip on the old cat Rus was feeling himself to be, and the notion that Gina would rub up against him and purr, and then follow him home, offer herself to him as his very own . . . well, that was more than a man could stand. At least this man.

It always had been a sentimental wish of his that his father preside over his wedding, and so he did three months before he died. Tongues wagged, but Lazarus Barden II's earthly home was now fixed. Two daughters followed. For five years Gina was his brown sugar, her body so familiar to him, such a comfort, awaking notions of lust and private pleasures of which he had not even dared to dream. Rus saw Gina as a rough-hewn natural thing, all limbs and mouth and hair, skinny like a teenager, but curvy where it counted. Her big eyes were at once a mystery and a blessing. (He serenaded her with an old Rodgers and Hart tune, and when she told him she'd never heard it before, that made his heart ooze all sorts of fluids. He discovered after they had wed that she had not ever left the state of North Carolina.)

Five years. Had it really been five years of connubial bliss, or five years he was so tightly wound up in his own fantasies of finally having achieved domestic harmony, all those American dreams and delusions and pretty pictures, magazine-quality, up on movie screens, IMAX big and tear-inducing, all those narratives we tell ourselves to sew our selves into ourselves, that he dismissed anything that did not fit in the film he was playing in his head?

When the sheriff walked in Rus almost didn't recognize him. Not that he looked much different—he had aged gracefully, and aside from his salt-and-pepper hair, had not gained much weight at all since high school, and his Melungean features were still firm, his teeth still horse-big and chalk-white. Rus began to wonder if he was making a mistake by coming here.

The first time Rus met Cavanaugh was in the fourth grade.

That year the schools of York County had finally integrated. The colored children eyed the white children, and the white children eyed the colored children. Nothing memorable occurred in those first days, everyone so intimidated by the new. But that very first day Cavanaugh kept peering at Rus's lunch box: a square box of aluminum inherited from his older brother, colorfully emblazoned with THE MIGHTY THOR, the blond god and his hammer and billowing red cape. Near the end of recess that day he walked up to Rus and said: "In a fair fight, I bet Thor would whip Superman's butt." They shook on the matter and had been pretty good friends ever since. (It struck Rus out of the blue: Why had his father allowed them to own a lunch box with a false god plastered all over it? A Baptist minister? But that just showed how little atten-tion their father paid them, and besides, what would he have known about comic books?)

They had played junior varsity basketball together, had run track together, but after high school Tony and Lazarus had only seen each other in passing, speaking, perhaps exchang-ing brief inquiries, at the Piggly Wiggly or the Walmart. "Hey, Freda," the sheriff Tony Cavanaugh said as he walked in the door, over to her desk, and picked up his pink message slips. "The world come to an end while I was gone?"

"I wish," Alfreda said. "Reverend Barden here wanted to see you."

The two men greeted one another with that perfunctory alacrity reserved only for old schoolmates, an admixture of nostalgia, genuine affection, personal comparison, and a bit of wariness. "Come on in." Tony led the way to his office. Surprisingly bare, save a large metal desk, no windows, not

79

even a carpet on the brick floor, only a cluttered corkboard behind the desk—Rus found this a dismal place for the chief law enforcement officer in the county to work.

"So what can I do for you, Rus?"

"Well, Tony. I did something—"

"By the way, man, you don't mind if I go ahead and start eating. I could eat a boar hog right now. Been here since five o'clock and didn't get to have any breakfast."

"No, no. Please. I don't mind at all. Please, go ahead."

"Want some?"

"No thank you."

Tony slid the foot-long sandwich from its clear plastic sleeve; he unwrapped the wrappings, releasing the scent of tomato sauce, a faint odor of cheese and new-baked bread. A meatball sandwich.

"Sorry, man. Go ahead. You were saying—"

"Yeah." Rus cleared his throat. "See. This morning I did something. Over at Possum Crossing. At the IGA. Well. I can't say I'm proud of it. But I'd do it again if I had the chance. And had to do it all over again."

Tony raised his hand, quickly swallowing, so as not to speak with his mouth full—"Man, what did you do?"

"I whipped J. C. Stokes with my belt. Figured I'd save you some time. Figured I'd turn myself in."

J. C. Stokes was a year older than Gina. Tall and rangy and dark—he worked off and on as a barber down on the marine base. He was loud and used profanity and seemed to have questionable hygiene. He was possessed of an overfondness for malt liquor, and when he was in the high cotton—and often when he was not—he favored Seagram's Seven with Coca-Cola. His musical tastes were stuck somewhere in the Ford, Carter, and first Reagan administrations—the Ohio Players, the Commodores, Rick James, Marvin Gaye: "When I get that feeling . . ." blasting from the rolled-down windows of his 1989 blue Chevrolet Caprice. He had lost his license so many times from Driving While Intoxicated convictions, he no longer even tried to reapply, taking his chance every time he got on the road, often with a bottle nestled betwixt his legs. He used words like "orientate" and "conversate," and "infer" when he meant "imply." He thought himself a great cook, and used his overpriced, gas-powered Weber grill outdoors twelve months out of a year. He used way too much salt, and always burnt the chicken, and usually everything else. Rus saw in JC's need to grill a reason to drink outdoors and to stay away from his Holy Roller wife. JC and this wife, Claudine, had only been wed for three days, right out of high school, when his car veered into a massive Peterbilt on Highway 41. The two were trapped inside for quite some time, and exposed to hellish flame. As a result they both suffered third-degree burns over most of their bodies. Both emerged from the hospital a few weeks later alive and disfigured. For Claudine, who was already in Abraham's bosom, this unfortunate event only made her more faithful, sweeter, more generous, the soul of Christian charity. But for JC, as the consensus in Tims Creek would have it, the crash had taken a wild boy and made him bad to the sternum.

He had never been a handsome boy, but his height, his sleek darkness, his long limbs, and something about his lips and the curve of his neck, made him a bit rakish to look at.

The burn scars, which ran down the right side of his body like lava, neither enhanced his appearance nor, in all honesty, detracted from it overmuch. The flamboyant wound seemed to make him a different person altogether, or merely to bring to the surface the wickedness that lay dormant all these years within him. Many pitied JC, saying his piratical behavior was the direct result of the tragic accident. Despite all the Christian charity Rus knew he carried around in his big ole heart, he could not find a way to care any less.

Some might say Gina and JC were the victims of bad timing. They had gone together all through high school, perpetually lip-locked and heavy-petting and wearing out Prince CDs while grinding. But when she discovered her long-legged lover on top of prim, Jesus-professing Claudine one fall night after a football game, Gina swore him off like cigarettes, and found solace in the arms of her first husband, a truck driver named Mike with a penchant for tequila, gambling, and drag racing. By the time that marriage had self-destructed, JC was actually in a rare month of seeking the Son of man. But when he awoke from his brief dream of redemption and had reacquainted himself with the Lord of the Flies, Gina was the bride of the Reverend Lazarus Barden II of First Baptist Tims Creek, 'til death did her part. This thing between Gina and JC was not love, it was an addiction. There were rumors as to how soon after Rus wed Gina that JC could be found in the pastor's bed. Rus chose not to mind the talk he might overhear, chalking that calumny up to hatefulness, to enjoying the misery of others. But as the years went by the two adulterers got downright sloppy. Rus had never caught JC in flagrante delicto, but there were clues, there were signs, like the phone call hang-ups when he answered, and the days and weeks that Gina would catch a mood and simply not speak to her husband, leaving him in doubt.

The phone calls were a fairly recent development in the scheme of things. To be sure, there had been calls that Gina took to the other room; the obvious codes when Rus could not be avoided; the one ring, followed by two rings, followed by Gina either making a phone call or going out.

Finally, last January, Rus simply replaced all the phones with new models all equipped with caller ID. When he got home the next day after work, Gina had restored all the old ones, saying the new ones weren't working right. The pastor and his wife had had their first fight in nine years. The calls continued, and suddenly with impunity. It was as if he were being goaded, tested, challenged. And for the life of him, he simply wanted this entire mess to go away. He wanted the woman he married to return. He wanted J. C. Stokes to vanish. He did not want any more unpleasantness. Yes, Jonah whispered his sin into the parson's ear, but inaction is sometimes action. Jesus would fix it, he told himself halfheartedly.

But last week. Last week. When the phone rang, rather than a hang-up, he heard a drunken and slurred voice. "Let me talk to Gina." "J. C. Stokes? What do you want? "I wanna talk to my woman."

"Don't you call here no more, boy. You get my meaning? And don't you ever let me hear tell you called, or let me see you sniffing around my womenfolk. Or, I hope God to kill me, I will—" "Shit," said JC, followed by a stream of babbling, incomprehensible at best, but Rus could make out "faggot" and "sonofabitch" and "cocksucker." He hung up. Within two minutes the phone was ringing again, or, more accurately, giving off its electronic, lonesome, and needy bleep. This time when Rus picked up there was just laughter on the other end. He unplugged the phone. God will not be mocked.

LAZARUS BARDEN II worked as an assistant director for MANPOWER for York County, finding work for the unemployed, the unskilled. He focused a lot on men recently released from prison. In many ways that job—counseling young men, helping them get a grip on life and a future, introducing them to hope, being a father figure who gave a damn—felt like his true ministry.

After college, he had tried a stint with the Merchant Marines and was happy he had been able to get out of that bargain quickly. He had knocked around in Washington and Baltimore until deciding to get his MBA, and as luck would have it, wound up working for an evangelist as a business manager. Why, in his early thirties, he decided to go to seminary escapes him to this day. Truth to tell, he often felt he had inherited his ministry, being the great-great-grandson of a minister, and the grandson and son of a minister, had given him no choice of letting his legacy down or picking up the mantle. But there were days now when he could admit to himself that resigning, throwing himself into a less Christ-haunted and more humane ministry, would suit him just fine. A drug counselor. A teacher. Or . . . he could simply abdicate. That word made him think of King Edward VIII and that Simpson woman. She would be something worth abdicating over. The thought of the Simpson woman made him think of Gina, and there arose in his gut a pang very like the beginning of gas. He enjoyed watching the History Channel.

At work these days he found himself logging onto the website of the Anchorage newspaper. His fantasy now was to abandon his life and move up there, to begin again. His cousin had worked on the pipeline in the 1970s, and ever since he heard those stories of moose and vast forests and mile-high mountains and bush pilots, he saw himself bundled in a bulky jacket, his face encircled by fur, woman-less, family-less, church-less, with nothing but the Bering Sea in front of him. His new destiny williwaw or bust. But that daydream felt even more like a fantasy than ever before.

IN TRUTH the potential humor in the situation had escaped him until he began to tell Tony Cavanaugh all the gory details, and he observed the sheriff becoming more and more animated between bites of his meatball sandwich, punctuating the narrative with: "What?" "You did what?" "And what did he do?" "No you didn't, bro." "Damn, Rus!"

If he had not run out of Tums, he would not have gone to the IGA food store in Possum Crossing, where they sold them, the cherry flavor with the calcium added, at a nice price, six to a pack. If he had not gone to the IGA, he would not have run into JC on the other side of the automatic swinging glass door. JC stood there, already drunk at 9:30 a.m., smelling unaccountably of sardines. They both stood facing each other for a while, drinking in the improbability of seeing just this fellow at just this time at just this place. JC—wobbling a bit on his feet—gave a smart-ass smile, which did not sit well at all with Lazarus. But he figured to ignore JC and walk past him, and to get on to his office in Crosstown, being already late. But JC did not move out of the doorway and nudged the pastor with his shoulder and looked right into Rus's eyes with his own bloodshot ones like a dog spoiling for a fight. Rus pushed past JC without much effort, though his manly place was already smarting a little. He could feel his throat go dry. After taking a few steps Rus heard: "Hey. Hey Barden. You stuck-up motherfucker. When I call your house next time, you damn well better put my woman on if you know what's good for you." Followed by a snicker, or something in that category.

Lazarus Barden II stopped under the awning to the store. It seemed something vital left him as he exhaled and something terrible entered him as he inhaled. It was a transmogrification, a possession, a quicksilver change. In his pause he lost touch with language. He only saw pictures at this point in his passage, he saw Gina, he saw his father, he saw his mother, he saw his girls; he saw wild horses and winged demons; he saw knives and buckets full of blood, and massive stones upon which entrails oozed and buzzards hissed. But prefigured and looming over all those icons and ur-shadows, he saw Jesus running the money changers from the Temple, and even larger, above it all, he saw the figure of Samson smiting one thousand and one Philistines with the jawbone of an ass. This all shot through his mind's eye with the speed of a synapse, so quickly the force was that of a vision, a prophecy, a heart attack.

He loosed and snaked out his long leather belt before he turned around. He gripped the buckle in his palm and looped the outside part once around the back of his hand, and advanced toward the taller man like a tennis player returning a serve. JC had little time to respond before Lazarus was upon him. The first blow to the face caused JC's eyes to bug with something like wonder and fear and disbelief, which only egged the pastor on, to convince the hateful sinner that what he beheld, what he felt, was indeed real. JC's hands flew up, instinctively, and within that same instant he began to weep and whimper at the same time. For a moment Rus held off the lashing, bemused initially, for he had fully expected a full-on fight, fists and whatever else need be swung. Instead he was met with a thirty-nine-year-old crybaby: *This is my cuckold? This is the man who wants to unman me? This is the fool who thinks he can do with me what he wants to do? This punk? This burnt-up child?* Lazarus brought down the belt with even more gusto. Again and again. To the neck, to the back, to the buttock, to the thigh. Now JC was on the ground. Now JC was writhing. Now JC was begging and hollering. The pastor was not parsimonious in parceling out his punishment. By and by, at some point, where exhaustion began to set in, and where fury began to wane, his superego came to the fore and said: *It is done.* Rus stopped, looked down at the man who dared to cuss him, to bang his wife and to brag about it, huffing and puffing as he was, and walked away. But within less than two steps his id, lounging in some newly liberated part of his brain, swigging a beer, spoke up and said: *Damn, that felt good. Give him a few more.* And he did.

But this time, after three whacks, Rus felt less righteous, less holy, less ordained to deliver this wrath. Less of a man, less of an avenging husband, less of a wronged individual. He paid attention for the first time to the crowd around him—a bag boy danced with glee, pumping his arms in the air, grinning broadly as if he had just witnessed a wrestling match on TV; Mrs. Abigal Johnson Jones, his mother's old friend, glared at him as if she were staring down the Antichrist himself, her mouth agape; two of the checkout women stood with their arms folded, their expressions implacable, only seeming to ask with their eyes: *Now what you gonna do?* And old Mr. Quincy, famous for being a centenarian and still driving himself, wheeled his grocery cart past the two men and said merely: Uh-huh. See there.

Of a sudden, tiredness enveloped Lazarus Barden. He needed to sit down. He wanted water to drink, but couldn't go back into the store. He dropped the belt to the pavement and strode to his car, not like a warrior who has vanquished someone of consequence, but very like a hunter who shot a fawn by mistake.

"Sounds to me like you thrashed him."

"Thrashed him?"

"Yeah, thrashed him. That's what you did. With your belt. You thrashed his ass, man. You know that reminds me. Remember Miss Holliwell from the fourth grade? She's got Parkinson's. Moved in with her daughter down in Charleston. Apparently her husband is a doctor and they got a big ole place on Fripp Island. The daughter and her husband, I mean. I used to like Miss Holliwell. She was always using words like 'thrash.' Remember?"

Rus nodded and waited. Tony consumed the balance of his meatball sandwich—there were only a few bites left—crumpled up the paper with a disquieting relish, and, mimicking an NBA player, launched the paper ball through the air into the wastebasket across the room. "Swoosh! Three points." Rus waited.

"Well," Tony said. "It was good to see you, Rus."

For a moment Lazarus Barden felt he was hearing another language. "Aren't you going to—?"

"Going to what?" Tony said, finally betraying a bit of impatience. "For what?"

"I imagine I broke a few laws, didn't I? Assault and battery? Something felonious."

"Well, sounds like you certainly did commit battery." Tony laughed a bit at his own wee joke. "But to tell you the truth, I don't give a rat's turd. Frankly. Sounds to me like that old fool had it coming. And I reckon I won't get voted out of office for letting the matter lay where Jesus flung it."

Tony stood up, and offered Rus a well-wiped hand, but did not look him in the eye. It was as if they both sensed intimacy was just not the apt thing at this moment. "Now get on to work or whatever you'd be doing this time of day. I got me some sheriffing to do."

OUTSIDE THE day was neither bright nor cloudy, just a rare and blessedly low-humidity spring late morning, the sort of Carolina morning to be envied. He wondered if the CVS carried belts, and thought to swing by there before he went into the office. As he pulled out of the parking lot, he heard the familiar and now dread *zzzzzzzzz zzzzzzzzz* and the telltale thump of his cell phone on vibrate doing its zombified dance across the car seat next to him. He could see on the tiny screen the caller: Tensy Barden. He just let it keep on buzzing. And buzzing. And buzzing.

Ezekiel
Saw
the Wheel

Gloria Brown dreamt her daughter would die in a helicopter. Tamar was a master sergeant in the army due to fly out for her third tour next Thursday. Tamar's birthday/going-away party was later that very day. Tamar's father, Gloria's ex-husband and business partner, would be there. Gloria needed to stop by and pick up the cake—a giant, rectangular-shaped red velvet cake, Tamar's favorite. Gloria kept glancing at the clock on the wall. She needed to go soon.

The man had sat in silence for the last ten minutes. Perhaps longer. Gloria was not really sure. But this sort of awkward silence was part of her job. Had been since the beginning. People would be surprised how often exactly this sort of thing happened. News of the recently deceased—especially someone mighty close—sometimes conjured up something like paralysis, as if the mind had gone off-line, had shut down to reboot. The man and his wife had been taking a long-postponed trip to the Outer Banks. The story was that she had kin there, though she had never met them, nor did they try to connect on this particular visit, and the couple had been on their way to Wilmington when she was stricken by a massive stroke at a Hardee's in Crosstown. The coroner had a "bug up my behind"—as he himself said one cold morning out back of the county offices, cigarette dangling from the corner of his mouth—about any corporate-run funeral homes, so he always contracted out to independents. Today he'd called Gloria and Ray, "Got an out-of-towner for y'all." What followed was paperwork, largely; a few phone calls; and an awkward conversation with a man who had not planned on driving home alone.

Gloria asked the man, who still sat in silence, "Is there someone I can call to come drive you back to Texas, sir?"

She could tell when it was about to happen, she could almost see it happening, like watching the lights at the top of a tower switching off, going dim right before her eyes. One level at a time. Radio silence. For some reason these silences never bothered her. Her ex-husband once told her she was simply intuitive and a natural empath. At the time Gloria had not a clue as to what he had meant. Gloria wanted to call the cake-maker to make sure the big red cake would be ready. She felt certain it would be, but she had a tendency to worry about things of this nature, things over which she had some control. Things like a grieving widower, for some reason, perturbed her much less. Indeed, she could tell he was not the sort of man who wanted someone to come and sit next to him, to hold his hand, and say those things a mortuary professional was expected to say, practiced, road-tested proverbs and reassurances as eye-catching and nonthreatening as fruit baskets, delivered with highly convincing sincerity which, paradoxically, could not be faked. Last night's dream had been in Technicolor, filled with swirling dust and lots of cussing. Big boys in big sand-colored boots. The sand-colored camouflage Gloria had come to hate seeing in airports. Anywhere. She dreamed a dream of blood. She dreamed a dream of helicopter blades going swoosh, swoosh, and swoosh, and then stopping. Just like in the movies Gloria had watched about the troops in Iraq. *Black Hawk Down. Jarhead.* That TV series on Lifetime. She had gone in and out of periods of watching and reading lots of media about the war. Some weeks she tried to pretend, tried to imagine Tamar was coaching basketball at a small school, or teaching, until she got an email from her daughter, or did that talking through the computer (that never seemed to work right), or it was time to send off a care package. In truth, she spent little time not thinking about her oldest daughter being 7,437 miles away from home, more or less. Thereabouts.

The dream tasted like reality and had the weight of the evidence of things not seen and the substance of things yet to come, and Gloria wanted to talk to her pastor, but her new pastor—the late Reverend Barden's replacement; all armed with his MDiv from Union Seminary and his MSW from Chapel Hill—would try to interpret the dream and talk about Alice Miller or some psychologist. Couldn't the man see she had been dealing with death and dreams for the last thirty years? She wasn't exactly a pullet. This sort of thing the pastor had done before. Gloria eventually stopped talking to him about her dreams. She knew when a dream was a dream and when a dream was more than a dream. This one felt like something more than a dream, and she knew there was not a thing she could do about it but pray. Tamar was getting on that plane. And Gloria was bound to see her off. Send her off. Cling to faith. See what the Lord had in store. Hope. Pray. Be humble. Believe.

Soon and very soon Gloria would finish up here with this gentleman, escort him out, finish making the transfer arrangements with the funeral home in Texas, lock up and fetch the red velvet cake. There was still plenty of time. She would arrive home to find her younger daughter, Eunice—so capable and reliable despite her seemingly silly and frivolous nature and inexhaustible need to gossip and her overweening need for attention. Her five children and her dour husband, happy only while watching basketball or football.

Gloria would find Lilith already in the kitchen, finishing up something delicious, something old, something new, show-ing off her almost supernatural skills, not so much a showing-off as an offering of herself, her abundance, an ingratiation: I am doing this, putting forth this effort, so that you will like me, Mrs. Brown, and there is so much to like; if you do not like me, something must be wrong with you.

Sometimes it took Gloria aback, startled her, when she considered how well she got along with—how much she actually liked and enjoyed—her older daughter Tamar's girlfriend—indeed thought of her as her own daughter, though in a guarded sense. Lord knows, in so many ways Lilith trumped either of her two girls as women . . . despite her affliction. But the Lord loved her just the same, the same as he loved Tamar. This lesson her new pastor was try-ing to teach her, had been teaching her, and what a blessing it was now to release the unease and vexation she had been harboring in her bosom, lo these many years. Since before Tamar played varsity basketball and all those loud whispers came from behind her back like coiled and poisonous vipers. But the Lord said you shall handle venomous snakes and yet live. Amen. This Gloria Brown had done. Many, many times.

Gloria sighed out loud. She grimaced when she realized she had troubled the silence. How long had they been sitting here?

Gloria imagined Lilith sitting where this abject Texan now sat. Gloria allowed herself to wonder how Lilith would process Tamar's demise. With cold, icy, machine-like efficiency? Or with the light, butterfly warmth that seemed to accompany almost anything she did, surrounded by doves, rainbows, and unicorns? Or would she suddenly reveal the seams in her stitchwork, unravel, allow the tears and the snot to run, and jump aboard the grief train full of howls and woe, incoherent and feeling the growing void inside? Or would she be like the stoic Texan before Gloria, incapable of speech, downright cataleptic with fear? Gloria knew that fear.

She prayed, *Lord, don't let my baby die over yonder. You are God and you send us signs and wonders, and your will shall be done. Your ways are not our ways. Your ways are mysterious and awesome to behold. But you said, Lord, yes you did, that the prayers of a righteous man—a righteous woman—avails much. Let no harm befall my girl, dear Lord, our Father. Protect her as you have protected her, and I shall remain your servant.*

The man was staring directly at Gloria, and for a moment she feared she had been praying in words and not just in her mind. As the stare continued unbroken, she knew it was something more, a recognition, something shared, something ineffable, very like the passing of an angel in the darkness of the night.

Listen.

Gloria Brown was very good at listening.

Mamiwata

for Dr. NCB

For as I crept deeper and the bush grew
denser and my heart sank lower . . . I
finally came upon a murky tributary of a
tributary . . . it teemed with such life . . .
toads, snapping turtles, and an unprece-
dented array of fish . . . And I decided this
place must be truly blessed . . . like Adam
I proposed to name it, like the mighty
river which begins in Scotland and flows
through . . . Oxford . . . Thames, as you
well know, meaning in Greek for senses . . .
At length I happened upon . . . a Negro
girl, standing on the bank.

> —from *Letters of Phineas Owen Cross,*
> *botanist* (1830–1921)

I've known rivers:
Ancient, dusky rivers.

> —from "The Negro Speaks of Rivers,"
> Langston Hughes

She took her time, walking like a fawn, careful not to make a twig snap. It was getting dark, but she could still see plenty. The voice grew and rose, and was the color of mint, like what Aunt Inez grew in a pot. Cool. Spearmint she called it.

She caught a glimpse of him, standing out in the middle of the creek, and he was quite a sight. Darker than she, with a wild head of hair. Big berry-dark lips. And his eyes seemed to flash in the dimming light. He was not exactly singing, more like humming, but in tune and to a rhythm foreign to her ears, yet familiar.

The water came up to his belly button, and he seemed to be doing nothing but standing there, in the water, humming and bathing, his dark skin glistening with water, and he spooned handfuls upon himself, humming his ditty.

"What you doing out yonder?" she called to him.

The man turned toward her with his flashing eyes and grinned in a playful fashion.

"Who you?" she said. "What you doing out there?"

"And who are you, little girl?" His voice was deep, deeper than Old Man Pharaoh's.

"I ain't no little girl."

The man waded closer to the shore, but stopped and said, "How old are you?"

"They tell me I'll be ten and four come the next moon."

She stood on the shore, he stood in the water, for a quantity of minutes eyeing each other, her with curiosity, him with placidity.

"What you doing out yonder then?"

"Standing watch."

"What you watching for?"

"You possess a great many questions for a fourteen-year-old girl."

"Aunt Inez says I got gumption."

"I suppose you do."

"Do you like catfish?"

"Who don't?"

"Another question. Come back tomorrow and I'll have one waiting for you."

"Where you live at?"

"Wherever I take a notion."

She grunted. It was getting dark, and she did not want to be down there at the creek's edge in the dark.

"You better come outta there, son."

"Why?"

"It ain't safe."

"You think you're safe where you are?"

"Safer than standing in that black creek. Ain't you 'fraid of gators and moccasins?"

"Not really. Come back tomorrow."

With that, she backed up, slowly, until her back came

against a tree. She turned and dashed up the trail. When she returned to the camp Aunt Inez stood by the kitchen.

"Where you been, gal?"

"I seen a rabbit. Went a-hunting it."

"You aim to catch a rabbit bare-handed, gal? You ain't never caught no rabbit, why you rabbit-crazed today?"

"Seemed like a smart thing to do."

"Girl, I have told you time and time again not to stray too far from camp. Alone without menfolk with you. You never know how far them dogs and catchers will come out here."

"You and Uncle Pharaoh say they ain't gonna come this far into the swamp."

"Ain't no telling. We always got to be ready to run." Aunt Inez looked her up and down, taking her all in. Amanda could not tell if she was approving or disapproving. The older woman sucked air in through her teeth. "Go fetch me a pail of rainwater from that barrel over there, and bring me more wood, and be quick about it."

It did at this point occur to her to tell Aunt Inez about the humming, bathing man out in the creek, but when she opened her mouth to speak, no words fell out. This worried her the way a mosquito bite worries. She went to fetch the water and the wood. She could smell the fish stew on the fire.

That night her dreams were populated by dark men with broad shoulders emerging from the creek. They were not nightmares, but they left her feeling uneasy and querulous inside. And to feel curious things in curious places.

The next day, after a breakfast of leftover fish stew and corn bread—the crawdads were even sweeter the next day—

she spent the morning splitting wood and weeding the corn rows. Aunt Inez sent her down to the creek to do some pot washing, with a cake of lye soap and a rag. She fully expected to see the man, but no man was there. All during her washing and scrubbing, she kept looking up and all about, but no man. Amanda felt the way she felt when Uncle Pharaoh didn't come back to camp after a visit back to the plantation. She lingered on the banks, but gave up, by and by, thinking hard thoughts of the well-made bather as she hauled the pots back to camp.

Rastus had caught a rabbit that morning, and Aunt Inez helped Mandy skin it. She allowed as how this was probably the rabbit she had seen the night before, a lie. Aunt Inez only moaned a moan neither in the affirmative nor in the negative, communicating that it did not matter one way or the other. 'Twas just the way things were. She now had another rabbit hide to tan and add to the quilt. Mandy loved to spend time rubbing her hand up and down the large tapestry of rabbit fur, black, brown, snow white, and mottled, so strong over you against the cold. Was a time she would feel bad for the murdered rabbits, but nowadays she got lost in the soft luxury of the thing. Plus rabbits were good eating. She could not deny it. But the quilt reminded her of pretty things the mistress owned back at Charybdis Plantation, expensive and lovely to the touch. Mandy did not like to think too much about the plantation. She reckoned she liked it better here. No. She did not reckon, she knew.

The sun commenced to go down, the shadows stretch out, and Mandy looked about for Aunt Inez, who was in the kitchen house, the smoke light as it tended to waft, and she snuck down the trail toward the water. A fat, long black snake crawled across the path a distance in front of her, and Mandy suddenly wished she had shoes, though she liked going barefoot when it was warm like it was. She heard the humming before she could see the water. She stopped stock-still. This time she decided to hide herself and fell to her knees and crawled into the thick cattails to the east of where the man bathed and hummed to himself.

He stopped humming. "Amanda. Why do you hide, child?"

Mandy stood up. "I ain't no child."

"But you are hiding?"

Arms akimbo, she asked: "Who is you, fool?"

The laughter was made of many things, and Mandy did not know what to think of it: Was he funning her, or was he just having fun? Was he happy out there all wet and fixing to get wet? Was he laughing because she called him a fool and he wasn't? It was a deep rolling laugh, the color of molasses, and his body shook. Ripples swam out from him in round wavy circles.

He stared straight at her, bobbing up and down, lightly like a stick. "I am one of you." Now he was still and staring at her. "I promised you a fish, didn't I?"

It rose up behind him without sound, no water slurps or splashes, slowly. So beautiful it was, see-through and bright. Two flat round things, almost like plates, a pointed tip sticking up at each top. It was bigger than his head, wider than his shoulders, and covered the all of him like a great big oak bough full with leaves. The thing shone in the fainting light, the last rays of the sun danced on it like pixies or fairies. It looked like it was waving at Mandy, gently, as if in a breeze, but there was no breeze.

A holler came up in Mandy's throat, but no sound leached out, only a puny grunt. And with that grunt the big thing flipped down into the water, made a scary loud SLAP against the flatness, and went under. The water behind the man seemed to boil and rumble. Directly it came back up with force and direction, over his head. And right in front of her, with a loud wet thud, there wiggled the largest catfish Mandy had ever seen in her life. She ran. She ran hard, and stopped behind a catalpa tree, tall and skinny, but wide enough to hide her small frame. She was breathing rough, and her heart was beating harder than even the night of the fire and the raid when she was taken away from quarters. That dark night full of flashes. Full of smoke and full of screams.

Mandy peeked out to see. The man was still standing there, grinning. The dog-sized catfish was still wriggling on the ground, its whiskers, each, looked longer than her legs; the mouth big enough to swallow her whole.

She struggled with it, carrying it in her arms, trying to avoid the whiskers, which looked mighty sharp. But it kept slipping from her grip and she kept having to stop to catch her breath. By the time she made it back to the catalpa tree, she stopped and looked back, but the fellow in the water had gone. Mandy felt angry with him. But was glad to be hauling back a big fish.

AUNT INEZ was the first to see her clambering up the trail with a beast slipping around in her arms. "Wheeooo!" Inez called out. Rastus came running and, much to Mandy's delight, lifted her slimy burden from her.

Uncle Pharaoh was standing there at the top of the trail. She knew what his return meant: he would commence to learn her the proper way to cipher and call letters as he did every time he returned to camp. Mandy was not exactly sure she enjoyed this reading and writing business, but she knew it was important to learn.

"You catch that fish, gal?" Uncle Pharaoh didn't look like he was either impressed or worried, just calm.

"Yes, sir, I did."

"Now why the Sam Hill you want to lie to me, child?"

"I'll tell you the plain truth, Uncle. That there catfish jumped straight outta the water, right high. Just as pretty as you please, and landed on dry land. Right at my feet. I ain't even seen nothing to beat it."

Pharaoh grunted the way annoyed bulls sometimes grunt.

By now Rastus and Inez had nailed the catfish down to a board, hacked off its head, and commenced to peel back the thick hide, which Rastus had to put great effort into doing. "I heard you talking to somebody out there by the creek earlier," Uncle Pharaoh said. "Who was it?"

"Just this fella, out there swimming."

"And you were gonna keep this a secret from the rest of us, were you? Was that your plan, Amanda?"

"No, sir."

"I assume he's a niggra like us."

"Yes, sir."

"He give you that catfish?"

"Yes, sir."

"It's a biggun."

Pharaoh joined Rastus and Inez, who were gutting the fish. "Looks like we got a friend."

"What you talking 'bout, Pharaoh?"

"Down by the creek. I prayed to her and she sent a friend."

"Now there you go again talking all that African foolishness," Inez said. "Ain't nobody believing in them overseas magic people but you, old man."

"How you reckon that skinny little gal catch a catfish that big?"

Aunt Inez sucked her teeth dismissively. "Mandy, go fetch me some water, gal!"

Upon her return Pharaoh put his hand on Amanda's head. "You need to be on the lookout all the time, gal. Especially when you wander away from camp. I ain't gonna try to clip your wings or nothing, but I need you to tell me you'll be careful. You hear?"

"Yes, sir."

THE NEXT DAY, Mandy had been itching to go down by the creek since she woke up, but figured she'd wait till the dimming of the day just like the other times.

This time as she approached the water she saw the man rise to the surface, headfirst. "Hey, Amanda."

"Hey yourself."

"Was the old fish good?"

"Sho'nuff." Mandy found it difficult to look him directly in the eye today. "What was that yesterday? That thing you brought up out of the water?"

"That was me."

"What you talking about, 'That was you'? What does that mean?"

Of a sudden the man cocked his head to the side at a peculiar angle. "*Sssshusssh*," he said, listening to Mandy did not know what.

"What's the—?"

"Be still, child."

"Wha—"

Sternly: "I said, *Be still!*"

By and by, she heard, in the distance, the baying of the dogs. Hounds no doubt, and a great crashing not too terrible far away, it sounded like.

"You need to come with me. Right now."

"I need to do what?"

"Don't be afraid, child, Amanda. I will protect you." The man spread his big arms wide open. And Mandy felt herself impressed by how wide they were.

Pharaoh always said they were bound to be found out, to always be ready to pick up and run deeper into the swamp. The dogs were getting closer and she could hear the voices of the catchers, hollering. She figured she couldn't run back to camp in time. Besides . . .

"Come to me, child. Get in the water."

Mandy could hear the dogs louder, closer, crashing through the brush. She peered into the woods to see what she could see.

"Mandy. You must come now! Time is a-wasting."

Mandy was not thinking as she dipped her bare foot into the water and stepped in. Not too cool. Not cool at all. Warm like rabbit fur. Warm like a belly full of hot chicken. Warm like a freshly picked ear of corn. Warm like a ripe tomato. Warm like Aunt Inez's hands.

Resurrection
Hardware
or,
Lard & Promises

for Alexa

I heard him before I felt his presence or saw him. A panting, a mild groaning as if from pain. I seem to remember a smell, a smell like an animal when in extreme fear—or perhaps that is simply something I filled in after thinking back upon that morning so many times. I do vividly remember the way the light poured in. The windows were all new and gleaming; the room a bone-white I'd admired and copied from certain museums I'd visited in the countryside of France. He was not hiding in the curtains, but rather on the floor, crouched, the gossamer fabric poorly hiding his dark skin. And he was so very dark. I could see him panting, his body not quite heaving but rising and falling as if in distress. A quilt, made by my mother, was folded at the foot of my bed. That is what I used to cover his nakedness and urge him into bed. He relented, eyeing me somewhat panicked, yet soothed by and by. I petted him, cradled him. After a spell I went down to make coffee and to think what to do.

When I returned with two steaming mugs he was gone. I've never had a problem sleeping in bright sunlight. Upon reawaking, I found the only evidence of his having been there—or of my believing he had been there—was the two mugs of cold coffee.

"It was a dream, brother."

I doubt it.

I

When the real estate agent first drove us up the gravel drive-way, I felt I'd been to this place before. I wasn't sure at once, for I'd first been there at night. Over fifteen years before. A dinner of academics after a lecture at UNC on Southern food. I was still living in New York then, and found the idea of living in a 203-year-old restored farmhouse out in the middle of nowhere surrounded by cornfields to be the height of fancy. Nothing in my future. Much too *Town & Country* for my tastes. Back then I fully expected to die on the twenty-first floor of a high-rise in the middle of some urban engine. How odd.

The two-story structure was still full of charm, not in the worst of shape but needed some serious love. That's how the agent put it.

Even though so much of the space was preordained back when John Adams or Thomas Jefferson was president, I was able to create a place I was more than happy to live and cook in. Especially the kitchen. Something in me feels immodest about falling in love with a kitchen I designed, but there it is. The deep stainless-steel counters, the tall glass-fronted cabinets, the Sub-Zero fridge, the six-burner gas range, the oven big enough for two large birds at once.

Immodest. Yes.

"I will never understand why you care so much about what other people think of you," Siddiq said.

"At this point I guess neither will I."

WE MET at the Harlem Settlement House, where I volunteered on Saturday mornings. He volunteered there as well. I taught a class in computer literacy to mildly interested brown and black girls whose parents had higher hopes for their futures. He taught a course on Islam. Fresh out of Brown University and full of socially conscious spirit. He invited me to coffee and we wound up at a rather bohemian place on the Upper West Side off Amsterdam, after a pleasant walk.

"Do you miss North Carolina?" Siddiq asked.

"Only when I'm there."

WHEN LENA Horne first went to Hollywood to make motion pictures, the studio hired Max Factor to create a makeup to make her appear darker onscreen. He called the cosmetic "Light Egyptian."

SIDDIQ WORE a halo of curly, rebellious long dark hair, and a rather piratical goatee. I wore one in those days myself, inspired by an Indian publisher.

He had a willowy build and large feet. His dark eyes shimmered in a playful way, and I could not help but imagine him in traditional Egyptian dress, and feel guilty for the fetishizing. He had perfected these long, long stares, held as if by a pharaoh. Some would find them imperious, rude, unsettling. I found them sexy, forward. He had the energy of a squirrel on amphetamines, and I imagined his lovemaking to be a fitful thing.

He allowed as how James Baldwin was his favorite writer. I allowed as how M. F. K. Fisher and Vertamae Smart-Grosvenor were mine. He then subjected me to an overlong disquisition on *Giovanni's Room* (he wrote his honors thesis on the novel). I took this as his signal to me that he was a same-sex loving man.

I told him about the house I grew up in on a farm in eastern North Carolina. I told him about my mother's career as a cook, and then a domestic and then a schoolteacher, and how she ignited my interest in food and language. I told him about my mother's gigantic garden. About Duplin County and school politics and altercations in the years just after forced integration. I had been in the first grade. About growing up poor, but well loved. And never ever hungry.

"Wow," he said. "You must be really angry."

"The arc of the moral universe is long, but it bends toward justice," I said.

He grinned, reached out his hand, and put it over mine. "Is that why you volunteer at the Settlement House?"

"It is a way to keep connected," I said.

"Do you feel disconnected?"

"So you're a psychoanalyst, are you? Doesn't everyone?"

"No, I'm not an analyst. But you are really, really guarded. I wonder what you are trying to hide."

LATER THAT afternoon, we wound up down at the Public Theater, one of my Saturday rituals. They showed foreign films in those days. Ariane Mnouchkine's 1978 *Molière*. Susan Sontag walked into the theater before us. That impressed him even more than it impressed me. It wasn't a celebrity thing, he said, it's a respect thing. Giuliani was mayor then. Clinton still in the White House. New York was experiencing a new type of hope and promise, or maybe it seems that way to me now because we were all so young then.

We had drinks afterward, in a quiet Village bistro-type café (he told me he did not feel comfortable in gay bars).

He took me to a tiny Haitian restaurant on Tenth Avenue. The waiter/owner greeted him by name, seemed happy to see him. She gave us a short list of specials for the day. He ordered pork, as did I. We launched into a delicious meal and a discussion of religion. His and mine.

His Egypt was not the boyhood of Anwar Sadat I had romanticized from having read the late president's autobiography, *In Search of Identity*, while in high school. No, that was his father's Egypt. Nasser was to Siddiq what Kennedy and Martin Luther King Jr. were to me. Myth. Sadat, a benevolent dictator who smoked a pipe. Siddiq was only eight when he was assassinated. He had grown up, not in a dusty village by the Nile, like his father, but in steel and glass towers, had been educated at private schools, summered in Sharm el-Sheikh, had been friendly with Mubarak's grandkids.

He had moved back to New York from university and still lived with his father and his two younger brothers in Carnegie Towers on East 87th Street. The first time I met his father—a rather good-looking man, smartly dressed— he was rushing to a meeting at the Saudi embassy. He had been a journalist, and was now the press secretary to a Saudi sheikh, the one who happened to be the Minister of Oil and Mineral Resources. He fussed with his cuff links, and paid me little attention. Siddiq had been keen on my seeing the view from their imposing bank of glass walls. "The sunset here. There is nothing like it. You can see Queens and Brooklyn and New Jersey."

"And Cape Verde if you squint."

When a thirty-six-year-old dates a twenty-four-year-old, the older man must learn to swallow his pride, and to discover he is proud in places he never knew he harbored it.

SEAN McGILLICUDDY was a big-boned, heavy-footed fellow of Scots-Irish extraction with hands like something made in a machine shop. His contractor business was based in Greensboro and he came recommended as a man who had experience with ancient dwellings. He roared with laughter when I told him what I was thinking for my budget.

"That might cover the kitchen," he said. "But you really want to redo all the wiring. That plumbing dates back to the early seventies. Just not up to code. And that roof. The windows. You'll freeze come November if you don't add more insulation, plus that's code now too."

Mr. McGillicuddy allowed Siddiq to help out with small tasks at first, and then to join in with the other workers. They were simpatico. McGillicuddy seemed fond of him. Though he tended to call him "Siddiqi." Praised his way with a hammer. Taught him how to cut Sheetrock.

"COME ON," Alexa said to me over the phone. "You know you've always wanted to do this, Randall. It will be fun. I'm going to call it *Lard & Promises*, all about Southern food, your beat. You'll have freedom. It's not like it was down here when you were a kid. I mean, my realtor is gay. Not your type . . . well, I mean he's pushing seventy, and white, but really. Come home, booboo. I need you."

Alexa found one of those Victorian brick former tobacco warehouses owned by the university, newly renovated, very near Brightleaf Square. I felt like I'd landed in an episode of *Thirtysomething*, surrounded by bright young, eager communications graduates, Brooklynites newly landed in Tobacco Row, not exactly bewildered, but stunned by Durham's heart and history.

My commute from Graham to Durham down Highway 70 charmed me, especially in spring, lined by redbud trees, dogwoods, and the occasional roadside vegetable stand.

We lived in her guesthouse while the house was being finished. She had come back to North Carolina a year before I did, and established her two children in an old lumber baron's estate just outside Durham. Alexa would visit my house renovation site on her own. She interjected her strong opinions. Dictated all the furniture choices, as was her style. I dutifully obeyed. Six months turned into a year. We moved in on a bright spring day. The downstairs bathroom was not quite finished, and some of the windows needed to be replaced, but . . .

"Well these sorts of things are never really complete, are they?"

I HAD seen him before. Before Siddiq left. He sat on the front porch in my new gleaming white rocking chair. I had been headed to the store and he sat there, eyeing me like a black snake. Calmly. Unmoving. Wearing what I took for homespun, but dingy. The weather had been warm so I thought nothing of his bare feet.

"Can I help you?"

"You live here?"

"Can I help you?"

"You live here?"

"Yes. I'm going into town. Can I give you a lift somewhere?"

He looked up, toward the cornfield, not too very far away. There stood a white man, dressed in black with a black hat, save for a white shirt and a large and quite brilliant white beard. He waved to the man sitting on my porch. It was a casual wave. The black man in white rose slowly and without apprehension and walked slowly toward the cornfield. They did not run, but simply walked away. Peculiar, I thought. I went inside and told Siddiq. Told him to keep his eyes peeled.

"Do what?"

"Just be careful. I need to go to the store. I'll be back in under an hour."

"But who is he?"

"I have no clue, baby."

"You remember that guy from Wrightsville Beach? He says he can take me on next week. He wants me to run his Surf City operation. Topsail Island."

"So you're leaving," I said.

"It's just till the end of the season. I'll be back."

"So you are leaving."

"Don't say it like that."

"What other way is there to say it?"

There had been a sign on the island, just after the bridge, inquiring after scuba instructors. Siddiq followed up. It seems you can't graduate from Brown without a master scuba diver certificate.

"Don't worry. I don't blame you. You'll have fun. Okay. Go ahead. Forget this old man and his old house. I wouldn't want you to be 'unfulfilled.'"

"Please stop being the martyr. You don't do that well. It looks bad on you. Trust me. I'll be back."

OF COURSE, he'd seen the Atlantic Ocean before, but something about the North Carolina coast spoke to him, seemed to beckon him.

Duck. Ocracoke. Hatteras Island. Bodie Island. Topsail Beach. Beaufort. Wrightsville Beach. Carolina Beach. Calabash. We took three weeks that summer. A car tour. Small hotels and motels. And I could see then that I'd lost him. How can you keep them down on the farm after they've seen the Hatteras Lighthouse?

A friend of mine likes to quote Isak Dinesen: "I know a cure for everything. Salt water."

For me it was the shrimp, the oysters, the mullet and the flounder and the red drum. Siddiq balked when he saw dolphin on the menu; I settled on the shark steak and he suggested I was a barbarian. I'm just hungry, I said.

SIDDIQ LEFT for Topsail in August.

Inder's email arrived in late September.

The dinner happened in October.

II

The house had gone through so much over the centuries, from the outside you would think it a modern edifice. Not so the barn. To look upon it was to think 1790. The logs had achieved that muddy gray color. They were practically petrified now. The structure was preternaturally solid. I only had to replace the roof. Even the stairs inside were firm, probably because they had been overbuilt to begin with. Initially I had planned to make a work-study and studio out there, but got overwhelmed by the reality of such a large renovation. So now we only used it for minor storage. It loomed significantly on the horizon of the property. It seemed to grin at me sometimes.

MY FIRST job right out of college had been for a 150-year-old glossy magazine of culture and lifestyle, *Tout Va Bien*. Alexa started at *Tout Va Bien* a year after I did.

Agnes Van Horne, the executive editor, was my boss. Agnes never stopped using a manual typewriter. She typed only on canary-yellow paper, triple-spaced everything, and used a soft-lead pencil to edit with bold heavy marks. She went over every line with the intensity of a gemologist. She taught me more about writing and editing than anyone.

"Darling, 'contend' is such a namby-pamby word. Never use it again."

I retyped all her copy, printed it out, and we'd go through the entire process again.

The magazine had recently undergone a new look, circulation was up, and Agnes remained in high spirits. I was still her assistant, long before I became food editor. Alexa had just finished her MFA, had hated Iowa. During the interview, Agnes spent a lot of time talking about Alexa's shoes. They got on famously from the start. Alexa began in the design department the next day.

ALEXANDER WAS a rude Princeton boy, straight out of central casting with his large hands and Clark Gable mien. Ten years our senior, I thought he was the quintessence of self-importance and entitlement. Though he did dress well. Who knows they want to become an arbitrageur at age fifteen? And who tells people that?

It was still the go-go eighties and Alexander was riding high. If you squinted at him sideways, you might mistake him for Gordon Gekko. And though I never once heard him say, "Greed is good," deep in his heart, I know he believed it.

"I thought you'd like him." Alexa frowned at me with a little pout.

"Why? Because he's hunky?" I asked. "The Savile Row suit, or that dashing splash of gray in his temple?"

"Oh, give me some credit."

"I do when you deserve it."

"You think I'm shallow when it comes to men."

"Everyone is, girl. It is a vocational hazard."

"You're just jealous. You want to bang him."

"I wouldn't kick him out of bed."

AFTER TWO fitful years of off-and-on dating, a trip to London, a trip to Greece, Alexa and Alexander were married. A surprisingly modest affair at the chapel of the Church Center for the United Nations, a reception in the West Village, not far from his brownstone ("It's not a real brownstone, you know. Not like the ones uptown").

Their marriage lasted seven years and seven months. Uncontested. All his fault.

NOBODY KNOWS how much she got in the divorce. I do. But the newspapers and gossip magazines only speculated. Most guesses I read were way off. A few added too many zeroes. Most lowballed it.

She moved back down South.

HER MOTHER had wanted to call it *Vittles*, and pouted when Alexa said, "Hell no, too straight-up folksy. People will laugh. Think it's a joke."

"I'm the publisher, and you're the executive editor, baby."

"Okay, Mrs. Lear."

We had both admired Frances Lear's short-lived magazine. She had taken her multimillion-dollar divorce settlement from Norman Lear, back in 1988, and decided to go into business for herself by starting a women's magazine. I always thought *Lear's* was beautiful and significant. So did Alexa. And we were equally fascinated by her and her elegance and intelligence and courage. We'd both accompanied Agnes to the launch party. We both had hoped to write for it one day. And were both sad when it closed down in 1994.

Hey, Randall,
I hope this finds you well. Ken and I are planning to
come to Chapel Hill next month. He hasn't been back

*since he graduated, and I have heard so much about
it from you two that I am dying to see it. Ron will be
coming in from Charlotte to join us, and a few of Ken's
friends from back in the day will be coming too. Will
you be free to join us for a drink, maybe even dinner? I
understand that you are busy these days with the magazine and all. But would love to see you, and this new
house you've been telling me about.
Give me a call when you get a chance.*

 xoxox
 Inder

AGNES ONCE told me a story about working for MacArthur
in Japan after the war. "Of course he was a Southern boy,
like you. Well not like you, but you know what I mean. From
Arkansas. Little Rock. Margaret and I would go out for sushi.
There was a charming little place not far from the Dai-ichi
Life Insurance Building, where we worked. This one had
managed to stay open throughout the war, despite the rice
rationing. Sushi wasn't as big a thing then, even in Japan,
as it is today. But he loved his steak and he had discovered
Wagyu beef, Mishima and Kobe, and he thought we were
mad. 'Raw fish!' Threatened to tell our parents. I tempted
him to try a nigiri once. He admitted it wasn't half bad. He
fed me a slice of his steak from his fork. Imagine that: the
Supreme Commander for the Allied Powers feeding me from
his fork like a little girl. 'Always bet on the beef, girl. Always
bet on the beef.'"

———

I'D GROWN curious about the history of the house and decided to do a little digging.

The Alamance County Historical Museum. Burlington. The Holt House dates back to 1790, but now is more Victorian in appearance. The outbuildings—an ancient kitchen, corncrib, and carriage house—were done up charmingly, as if no food had ever been cooked in the kitchen, no corn ever stored in the corncrib. I had called ahead, inquiring about the history of the place.

I don't know what I had expected. Maybe someone like my fourth-grade teacher, Mrs. Hollingsworth, a card-carrying member of the Daughters of the Confederacy with a thick, rich South Carolina accent, a bright print dress, and shoes too tight. But not this woman who could pass for the Duchess of Marlborough, transplanted but fiercely dedicated to the Southern past.

"So you bought the old place. I had heard the professor died."

"The professor?"

"Yes, didn't they tell you?" she asked in her minted Oxbridge accent. "Who sold the place to you? Probably that Ann Baxter, did she not? Yes, I should have guessed. She views local history as a nuisance. Only interested in McMansions and her fee."

The docent had come to the States as a military bride, back in the sixties. Her husband died in 1979, she told me.

"The professor?"

"Yes, William Gaddins. He taught at Carolina. History, of all things. He came here from Ann Arbor back in the seventies with three little girls. All grown-ups now. I don't know where they live. Well, Betsy, I do . . . Regardless. He raised the girls all alone, while restoring the old inn—"

"Inn? My house was an inn?"

"So she didn't tell you that either, I see. She probably has no clue. Yes, Mr. Kenan, that place was built in 1790. Did she tell you that? It was an inn run by Quakers. You see, a man-made canal snaked its way very near your back door, and by the mid-nineteenth century, a great deal of traffic came by there, down from Greensboro and Old Salem en route to Fayetteville and below. The canal was built to avoid the rocks of the Haw. People came to refer to it as a creek.

"A Quaker family ran the inn from the turn of the century until a few years before the Civil War. They seemed to vanish around 1860. No record of where they went or why or how. I have my theories, of course, but no evidence. You know Quakers were staunch abolitionists. Many were persecuted because of it. A great many were run off the land here.

"Again, I have no evidence. But I strongly believe that inn was used to smuggle slaves to freedom."

I thanked her and began to retreat to my car when she said: "You know they exterminated them."

"The slaves?" I asked.

"No." She gave me a sly grin. "Not by a long shot. The Quakers. You know they once owned most of this area. Daniel Boone's people. After the war—what my colleagues euphemistically refer to as 'the War of Northern Aggression.' They were practically all wiped out just before all that. Exterminated."

———

"COME LOOK at this."

Once upon a time I imagine there had been a door. But then again perhaps not. A false wall. A panel. A compartment smaller than a closet. I imagined a body or two cramped in there. I wondered for how long.

After I found this room the noises and lights started. Outside. Voices really, and the sounds of feet trudging around in the yard. Murmurings each to each, and the lights flickered as if by flame. I did not rush out to discover who it might be, and when I peeked out the window the lights were doused.

Siddiq regarded me with the look a teenager gives to an older person they do not respect yet refrain from ridiculing while thinking some proper answer will come.

"These things do not happen in Egypt."

"Oh, quit lying."

"They do not."

"YOU'RE COOKING a what?" Alexa was fascinated by the "reunion." "A goose? Are you mental?"

"How long have you known me?"

"Are you getting it from Stone Creek?"

"No, a place called Elena's Farm in Thomasville. Will you come?"

"I have to be in Asheville that day. Maybe I'll stop by on the way back. What kind of sauce?"

"I was thinking port, cherries, and ginger. Potatoes. Brussels sprouts—roasted too, of course. Sweet potato tarts." I intended to cook Inder and his new husband a good meal.

"You are such a fool."

"That is why you love me, bitch."

I HAD met Inder through an old-school, truly primitive computer dating service, back in the late eighties. I was assistant food editor then. My best buddy at the time suggested we go in on it together. We were both single, both somewhat on the make, both lusty and able, both spending too many fruitless weekends in the bars and clubs.

He showed me the ads in the *Village Voice*. "Let's try it. What have we got to lose?"

"Twenty-five dollars."

"Don't be so damn negative. You spend that on drinks at Uncle Charlie's in two hours."

We filled out the forms and waited.

Six weeks later my results arrived in a thick packet, spooled computer paper, dot-matrix printouts, seventeen or so matches. Only a handful seemed even remotely promising. I went through with it on a dare, and called three. I met the first two guys and was sorely disappointed. (Perhaps they were equally so.) But the third, as they say, was a charm.

Inder was a Punjabi Sikh, a twenty-something medical intern, working at Kings County Hospital, where I had been born. At the time, he was preparing to be in his sister's wedding, and sported a long, dramatic beard, as was the custom in Sikh weddings. By 1988 the hospital was a sprawling complex including dormitories, and I could not help but reflect upon the idea of making love in the place where I had been born.

I ended the thing rather abruptly after a season. For no

other reason than I was quixotic then—as I am now—and felt too hemmed in. And yet some of my favorite memories ever:

Cooking alongside his mother in their Brooklyn flat, my first home-cooked Indian food.

Attending this sister's wedding, also a first. It felt more like a festival than a wedding reception. Music, dancing, food galore.

We are made by the things we regret.

MY FIRST year of college, I lived on the North Campus in Chapel Hill surrounded by prep school boys drunk on ska, punk, and reggae. Alexa had grown up on Florida's Space Coast to a prepper father, long before survival-style lifestyles were a fad or a word. She lived on South Campus and happily only associated with black folks. I made a beeline for New York when she went off to Iowa. On fall and spring breaks she would come visit, and amid walks on the Promenade, across the Brooklyn Bridge, or ambling about Prospect Park, she fell in love with Brooklyn.

"Guess what, Alexa? I met Alfred Kazin."

"Of course you did."

I FOUND a patch of periwinkle at the edge of my property where the cornfield meets the wooded area. It was close to a fourth of an acre, I would guess.

I remembered having read that the graves of the enslaved were often marked only with periwinkle to keep the ground free from all else.

KEN WAS the one I feared meeting. I did not remember him at all, and wondered if I ever truly had met him as an undergrad. He had been a cheerleader, and I never went to home games. Pictures aplenty of him abounded, of him in the cheerleader outfits, of him and his gals and guys making the classic human pyramid. Standing on the yard line at the football stadium, a sea of sky-blue-and-white-clad humanity, an improbable grin upon his face. The only black male in the crew, and two black women, in a team of twenty.

While I was getting coffee for Agnes Van Horne and sleeping with his future husband, he was getting his master's from Harvard's vaunted Kennedy School, going on to a fast-track career in telecommunications. He was now a vice president for what was still Pacific Bell.

The thing you want to know, the thing you don't want to know.

AND THEN there was Ron. Ron and Ken had remained close over the years. Ron was only one of two men I tried to seduce via poetry while an undergraduate. Though the poems were embarrassingly earnest (I should quote some here, but I am mortified by it now), he spoke to me nicely after reading my Shakespearean efforts, and told me he thought I had talent. The fact that he had absolutely positively no romantic interest in me was as plain as a dick on a donkey. Ron was now the principal of a large high school in Charlotte. Inder told me he was dating a tall white leatherman, and that Ron had a penchant for S/M and kink. He was still a beautiful man.

"JUST BE sure to keep it niche," Sidney kept saying to me and Alexa. Sidney was the business manager. He remained in New York, where he ran a small crew of marketing and sales people. Alexa decided she would be her own art director, having done it professionally for so many years, photography and design being her main passion. So she left the niche-ifying to me. Our goal was to land the thing somewhere between *Southern Living* and *The Believer*—I had hipsters on my sonar, and every time I said "hipster," I could hear the grin in Sidney's voice. To be sure, all the folk we were able to hire, and who got what we were trying to do, fell into the nonhipster-hipster category (for we all know, no one is a self-proclaimed hipster). Each of them had forgotten more about craft beer than I would ever learn.

There were the requisite interviews with the hot, up-and-coming young chefs of the moment, but one of my favorite things was a series of interviews with noncook cooks. An Atlanta DJ's choice of comfort foods; a Jacksonville truck driver's go-to self-packed lunch; a Paris Island drill instructor's best home-cooked meal. I had just completed an oral history of the white women who worked at the Greensboro Woolworth's counter at the time of the 1960 sit-ins. When I told them I worked for *Lard & Promises*, they wouldn't stop talking.

We started at a bar on Henderson Street. A place, when we were undergraduates, known to have gay Thursday nights. Chapel Hill having no real gay bars, then or now. That night it was damn near empty, when I met all six of them there at the bar. "You look good, man," Ron said, and asked what I would have to drink.

Inder hugged me, and introduced me to his husband. Ken hugged me too, and acted as if he remembered me. I followed suit, knowing it was a lie.

The night droned on, a night at moments threatening to be boring, but Ron and his allegro spirit always managed to lift the dark rum to tequila lemonade, which was perhaps one of the reasons I'd become infatuated with him from the start. The bar DJ—or whoever—played a mix of tunes from gold to old, Chaka Khan met Kanye West met Stevie Nicks met James Taylor met Missy Elliott. And after a few beers I felt myself silly, wondering what I had set myself up for. Remembering a short story by John Updike about a fifty-year high school reunion: they are never what we build them up to be. We expect some grand revelation. Revelations work on their own time, not ours. The beats beat on. The night beat on.

"You writing any poems these days?" Ron had a wonderful way of dominating a conversation, a gathering. Not in an obnoxious way, but in a reassuring, avuncular, fun way. "Not in fifteen years, I think."

"That's a pity. You got the soul of a poet."

"Yeah? Tell that to my boyfriend."

"He ain't a poet?"

"No sir."

"What is he?"

"Pretty. Smart. Egyptian."

"Uncut?"

"He was born a Muslim, silly."

"Oh." Mischief danced in his brown eyes.

I took a deep quaff of a Guinness which I had no business drinking. "Look, there is some weird shit going on at this house I bought, and—"

"Let's go, guys!" Ken announced rather loudly with the

authority of a senior executive vice president. "Let's take a walk."

Ken wanted Inder to see the Old Well. They'd already toured South Campus and the Dean Dome. Now it was the Bell Tower, Wilson Library. Silent Sam, the dubious old Confederate statue who guarded the entrance to the campus. Talk about ghosts.

We ended the evening at the Carolina Inn, where they were staying, drinking prosecco and arguing about the "death tax."

"Okay, guys," I said when I noticed how late it was getting. "See you tomorrow. About seven p.m., right."

"I got the address in my GPS." Ken waved his phone at me.

"Be sure the number is in there too. My place is out in the boonies."

THREE DAYS after we first moved in: three o'clock. Someone violently banging at the back door. Can the heart beat any harder? I have read that our reactions in such moments are completely involuntary. Sounds bypass the brain and go directly to our spines.

"Who the hell is it?"

The banging stopped. I wished the back door had a window at the moment. I could see through the side window that the motion-activated floodlight was on. Should I open the door?

I had a gun, but kept forgetting to get buckshot for it. So I picked up the machete I kept behind the door. Perhaps knowing Siddiq was upstairs emboldened me; perhaps I'd drunk too much scotch.

There was no correct way to open the door, rather than to yell and swing it open at the same time. No one was there. I could hear Siddiq's bare feet coming downstairs. I saw the barn door open, a faint light within.

Machete in hand, I marched barefoot across the gravel and grass to the ancient barn. I imagined I looked like some figure from a 1950s zombie movie. As a student of modern Russian history, I have always conjured up an image of what the czar's family looked like the moment after their ignoble assassination. Of course we don't have to imagine it—we have photographs. The sight in my barn was akin to that. The man in black, a woman in a black dress, three girls all askew, and a boy-soon-to-be-a-man. All expired, all teetota-ciously exflunctified. Siddiq's wail came up from behind me, incredulous. Horrified. I know he saw it too. I heard him running back to the house.

I closed and bolted the barn door before even thinking to call the police, which I did not. Knowing the scene would be gone by daylight. Which it was.

"Who is it? What do you want?"

THE PHONE RINGS, wakes me up. The night of the first gathering in Chapel Hill.

It is Siddiq. "What's going on? Are you okay?"

"I'm just fine."

"Are you ready for tomorrow?"

"Everything is ready. They'll be here at seven."

"And the house?"

"Mr. McGillicuddy finished up on the windows last week."

"You know what I mean . . . anything . . . ?"

I was silent. Then let out a long, dismissive sigh.

"So what was it like, seeing those guys again?"

I narrated the evening. He stayed silent.

"Okay. I just thought I'd check in."

"How thoughtful of you."

"Right."

III

The goose came out just fine—succulent, flavorful, the fat a thing of pure joy. My sauce, not too sweet yet tangy. I was happy with my decision to use so much ginger. The potatoes were overdone, but an overcooked potato is not the end of civilization. The Brussels sprouts made me proudest, which is silly. But their consistency, their texture, the crunch, the amount of doneness made me exceedingly happy.

"This turkey is weird," said Ron.

"I think Randall said it's goose," Ken said.

"Oh, that's why. That makes sense. Kinda greasy, ain't it?"

"I think it's delicious," Inder said, and gave me the look he gave me when he beheld me cooking in the kitchen with his mother in Brooklyn back in 1988.

"Where's your Light Egyptian, man? Inder told me you were living with this pretty boy. Where he at?"

"Topsail Beach."

"What the hell he doing down there? Why ain't he here?"

"It just be like that sometimes, don't it?"

"He's missing some good vittles. Damn! Pass me some more of them potatoes, son."

Before dessert Ron excused himself to the bathroom. I cleared the table, poured more wine, and began setting out the sweet potato tarts. Ron returned. "Why is there a naked man in the bathroom?"

"What man?"

"Ron? Are you—"

"I'm serious, man."

I knew he had seen him, I knew he was telling the truth, but I was distracted by how calm he was, supernatural phenomenon or not. But that was so Ron.

A knock at the door. Timing, as the man said, is everything.

Alexa rushed in like a subway into the station. "Sorry I'm late. Already on to dessert, huh? Good. Where's the goose? I know you saved some for me. I want me some goose. I've been thinking about goose all damn day. I'm thinking we can do a piece about goose farming. What do you think?"

All the men stood round the table, made from one of those planks found in the house, no doubt from a tree planted back in the eighteenth century. Their eyes told a story seemingly as old.

"Okay. What the hell happened? Why are you all looking at me like I just walked into an orgy uninvited?"

"Naked Negro. Bathroom," Ron said, and shrugged and picked up a dried cherry and commenced to chew. He motioned to the bathroom.

Alexa spun on her heels, in that imperious fashion that made her. I could see in her Agnes Van Horne, Frances Lear, and Alexa. She marched to the bathroom and swung the door open.

"Okay. So what y'all been drinking?"

I inspected. Ron inspected. Inder and Ken inspected. Ron ate his tart, poured more wine.

BEING THE only woman in a party of gay black men was just Alexa's style. She was right in the mix instantly, as if they'd all been old friends. Though we'd all gone to school together, she had run with a different crowd.

RON GAVE me a look I sometimes got from my pastor when I was a boy asking stupid questions like, Who is God's mother? "So let me get this right: you moved back home with this pretty boy intending to play house in this old place out in the middle of nowhere and live happily after ever. Is that the idea?"

"I reckon," I said.

"You can't always get what you want, brother."

"Wasn't it Frederick Douglass who said: 'You may not get what you pay for in this world, but you will certainly pay for what you get.'"

"Yeah, he said that and a whole lot of other shit."

"I'm okay. Really. Truly. I'll be fine."

"Yeah, just haunted."

CODA

Do ghosts eat? I make breakfast for two. Perhaps from sheer force of habit. Yet another day without Siddiq.

My visitor, my new friend, sits at the table with me. He seems to admire his plate of food, but does not eat.

I hear a bell in the distance.

Opening the door: it is fall, but spring outside. I see a completely different landscape. The trees all full of leaves. Abundant green, blindingly bright sunshine, butterflies, flowers. All that buzzing. I see the creek so much closer than I expected. And there is a wooden dock. I see a different world.

I see a long flatboat approaching. The creek is not much more than a ditch, not much wider than the boat. I see a man, a white man, heavy and full-bearded, coming our way, moving the boat along with a long tall wooden pole. My friend seems to be both relaxed and eager. The boatman waves, and calls out, "Oye!" I wave back, and my friend waves back. By and by, the flatboat docks, and the two of us go out, me in my pajamas, my friend totally nude. The boatman greets us, and I think of Greek mythology, till his warm hairy hand grasps mine, and he says, "We need to get a-going. Seen two patrollers on horseback a few miles back, but past Greensboro, I reckon. Can't be too careful now." My friend clambers aboard and looks upon me, expectantly. The boatman situations him among a number of wooden barrels, bids my friend to crouch among them, and then spreads a broad, rough canvas over him. "Get on in," the boatman says to me, eager to shove off. "I think I'm good where I am," I say.

The boatman spits absently. "It's your funeral, brother. Take your chances. I know they're a-coming."

"I will be fine."

The boat launches and heads south. "Take care of yourself, brother. May Jesus and his angels bring you to safety."

My friend pokes his arms and head up from the canvas. He waves to me. It is one of the most free-hearted and brotherly waves I have ever witnessed, full-armed, vigorous. A form of communication surely only known to the first humans. I wave back, I stand and watch them disappear round the bend of the channel. A dragonfly lands on the dock. The beating of its wings is loud to my ears.

I go back in and enjoy my ham, grits, and red-eye gravy and scrambled eggs. I think of my mother, I think of my lover, I think of home.

The Acts of
Velmajean
Swearington Hoyt
and the
New City of God

She kept peeking through the blinds to see if they were still there, as if the situation had changed in a mere five minutes. Every time she would see the vans with their gigantic white mushroom antennas sprouting up toward heaven. CNN. NBC. MSNBC. FOX. BBC. CBS. BET. Piney View Lane had been clogged and coagulated with people and cars. The Orange Grove police had erected barricades and had taped off her yard with that yellow police tape Velmajean remembered from television police shows. But seeing the brethren—some full-time security, some volunteers from the church—made Velmajean breathe more easily. The sight of them reminded her that the Reverend was in charge. And he was going to make sure everything would be all right. Any minute now he would be arriving for the press conference where they would announce Velmajean's next miracle.

On one of her compulsive peeking trips she was happy to see the Reverend's sleek black SUV pull up, a miracle in and of itself the way the crowd parted before it like the Red Sea for the children of Israel. It was one of those bright autumn days in North Carolina where the leaves swirl about like roan pixies. At first the sea of reporters engulfed the arriving dignitary, but thanks to the brethren a path was made, the tape was lifted, and an entourage from the church made its way to the house. Before he could knock, Velmajean opened the door.

"Oh, Reverend, I can't tell you how glad I am to see you."

The Reverend Jamie "Spike" Eggleston took off his shades, paused in his patented way, and opened his arms to the sixty-two-year-old widow. He flashed his cover-boy smile, which always made Velmajean more than a little giddy and wrong-feeling inside. It was the sort of smile that could cause her to write bad checks. "Sister Velma, how's our little miracle worker?"

As they embraced, and the Reverend whispered calming, dulcet-toned words into her ear, in filed five men: two lawyers and three equally suit-clad bodyguards. The Reverend himself was in his usual jeans and signature formfitting sweater. He was easily the largest man in the room, and his muscles visibly undulated underneath each time he moved. "Sister, the Lord's got big—*big*—things in store for you. Hallelujah." He slapped his hands together with a loud slap, as if he were about to close some great deal. "Hallelujah." That was one of the Reverend's favorite words. He used it the way gang members used the F-word. He looked into her eyes, expectant perhaps for confirmation or outburst or questions or doubt. But Velmajean simply smiled. She wanted to get this ordeal over with. *General Hospital* was coming on in ninety minutes.

The Reverend Spike ordered everyone to get down on their knees. The men encircled Velmajean Swearington Hoyt, placing their hands on her shoulders and back, the minister laid his hand on her forehead. He said: "Father God.

Please bless this endeavor into which we—your children—are about to embark . . ."

"Praise God," said one of the bodyguards.

". . . and please guide my tongue . . ."

". . . guide him, Lord . . ."

". . . for the further glorification of your kingdom. We ask a special prayer for your chosen vessel, our sweet sister Velma here, Lord. Hallelujah. That her heart remain pure . . ."

". . . pure . . ."

". . . and that you continue to use her as your sign upon this earth."

"Amen."

With that, the men helped Velmajean to her feet.

"Do I look all right, Reverend? I mean will this look okay on TV?" She wore a sky-blue dress of conservative cut from the collection of one of her favorite designers that she'd bought at Hecht's department store a year ago. One of the women from the church had come by and touched up her silver coiffure. Again the Reverend Spike looked at her as if she were the kumquat of his eye, the center of his universe. "You look positively radiant, sister."

With that, led by the Reverend, followed immediately by Velmajean, and then the five men, the group marched down the path from the split-level brick and beige house, built in 1976 and paid for in full by the death of Velmajean's husband, Parker Hoyt, in 1996, down to the horde and the lights in the middle of that Thursday afternoon, to the microphones feeding up to satellites informing televisions and radios and computers around the globe; and where the Reverend Spike Eggleston, the former Internet millionaire turned Christian entrepreneur, announced that on the coming Sunday at a special service to be held at the newly completed Atomic Church of God and Worship Center ("congregation 20,000"), Mrs. Velmajean Swearington Hoyt of Orange Grove Township would be doing the Lord's work, "by performing her thirteenth recorded miracle live on an international broadcast sure to reach two billion people, to convince them of the Almighty's presence in the world and in their lives."

Just as the Reverend had instructed, Velmajean stood and smiled for no more than two and a half minutes for the flickering barrage of lights, never uttering a word, whereupon two of the bodyguards escorted her back into her well-guarded four-bedroom home, while the Reverend and his lawyers fielded questions for another twenty-seven minutes.

Velmajean considered watching the show on TV, but reckoned it would be on—in an edited version—in heavy rotation well into the night.

As she took off her dress, looking forward to relaxing, to trying to put all this hoopla out of her thinking, she realized with a start that she recognized a face in the crowd. That strange, beautiful man she had seen that day in the parking lot, the day she brought the little girl back from "the other side."

THAT DAY had been a Thursday too, and she had gotten to the supermarket early. She was feeling particularly proud of herself, for with the judicious and meticulous use of coupons, she had purchased $201.29 worth of food for $79.82 ($25.25 would be in rebates).

As she labored to put the groceries into her six-year-old Oldsmobile—once upon a time bag boys offered to help, but those days were long gone—a young man walked up. "Please," he said. "Allow me."

"Thank you, young fellow." She was pleased and flattered. He was black—an African, blue-black—and basketball-player tall. He was smartly dressed in a black suit, over which he wore a long black coat that almost touched the ground—odd on a pretty spring day. And he wore shades. His head was clean as an eight ball and just as dark. For some reason he reminded her of the Secret Service agents who surround the president, and for that reason, or so she reasoned, she felt safe around him.

When he was done he closed the trunk. The grocery cart was gone.

"Where—"

"You are blessed among women, Velmajean Swearington."

At first, so perplexed by the disappearance of the cart, she had not registered what he had said. She looked at her African chieftain in his expensive suit. "Yes, young man, I know. Have we met?"

"No," he said, "I mean you are truly blessed."

With that, he reached out and took her hand. The feeling was warm at first, then noticeably hot, her hand tingled, her face flushed. She could not move, only stare at the stranger. To this day she could not swear on exactly what it was she felt, only that it felt better than sex, sweeter than love, stronger than the will to live. Or maybe it was just the spring air and his warm hand and smiling face.

Just as quickly the man let go and stepped back. He spoke only one sentence after that, before he walked off into the highway to melt into the traffic as if he were some human sports car.

He had said: "His wonders to behold."

Looking back on it, Velmajean marveled at how easily she had brushed the entire incident aside. Laughed it off. Thought nothing of it. Straightaway. *Good Lord*, she had told herself, *there are some crazy folk walking around here.* As for the touch: He sure was warm-blooded.

Perhaps, again in hindsight, she might have thought on it more had she not, no more than twenty minutes later, turned onto Kensington Road: a beige Suburban SUV overturned. An ancient Dodge Dart on its side, the wheels still rotating. A man, distraught, standing, pacing. A man and a woman on their knees. Lying prostrate and motionless before them a child, bloody and twisted.

Velmajean rushed from her car and toward the people as if by instinct. "Oh, no. Oh, no."

Both the woman and the man were crying and clutching each other, a portrait of kneeling sorrow; pitiful, tear-soaked visages, bodies quivering with sobs. The standing, hippie-looking man, his long hair flaring out in all directions, was possessed by a wild look of despair. "I didn't see your turn signal, man. I didn't—Oh God. I didn't—"

Velmajean had been ordered to take rudimentary first aid and emergency skills classes as part of her job as office manager at Deco Furniture long before she retired. She asked if an ambulance had been called. If the girl had been moved. No one answered her.

She knew to check for vital signs: the eyes, the breath, the pulse. At first things seemed dire. There was a lot of blood. She could not see where the blood was coming from. But as she touched the girl, by and by, the little one began to stir. First her leg, and then a piercing cough. With flutters the girl's eyes opened, and she lifted her head, at first tentatively, and then with the full strength of youth. "Daddy?" She began to cry.

"Oh my God!" The woman grabbed the girl up into her arms. The man literally yelled.

"She must have just been knocked out. But don't move her," Velmajean said.

"No," the man finally said, as he too rushed to his daughter. "She was dead. She was dead."

"You must have been mistaken. See. She's right as rain."

Down on her knees next to the father, both smothering their daughter in hugs and sobs, the mother finally raised her head and said: "You don't understand. My husband's a dermatologist. She was dead."

Still and all Velmajean drove off that day convinced that things were never as bad as they looked.

VELMAJEAN SWEARINGTON HOYT had belonged to the St. Thomas Baptist Church of Orange Grove Township all her life. In her youth the church, just outside Durham, had been thriving, the center of a small crossroads community not even listed on most maps. The minister, the Reverend T. T. Bryant, had been a theology professor at Wake Forest Seminary, and had as much charisma and warmth as he had theological knowledge and wisdom. Folk always said his sermons were like an angel's home cooking. Velmajean had been baptized in that church, she had been married in that church, and both her parents, and finally her husband, had been funeralized in that church.

By that time the congregation had dwindled almost to the point of extinction. The community had been engulfed by building, and what had once been a village on the outskirts of a small North Carolina city had become a bedroom community full of apartment complexes and strip malls and oil change shops, grocery stores, fast-food restaurants, movie theaters, and gas stations. When, at the ripe old age of ninety-three, the Reverend Bryant passed on to his reward, the board of trustees were faced with a sad fact. They only had seven members left. All of them sitting in the same room with a lone real estate agent who had a bad hunger for land, the land under their church. Now, seven years later, where St. Thomas Baptist Church once stood loomed a vast car dealership shaped like a hog.

For several years Velmajean wandered from church to church on Sunday mornings looking for what people called a "spiritual home." She preferred to call it a church. She had tried the high-toned, Sunday-go-to-meeting Baptists, the speaking-in-tongues Holy Rollers of the Pentecostal, the casserole-toting Methodists, the choir-besotted AME Zionists, the hat-happy Church of God in Christs—but none of them felt right to her, felt comfortable. Each was like a pair of shoes she admired until she tried them on.

One fine Saturday morning there came a knock at Velmajean's door. There before her stood that nice couple who lived five doors down, Philip and Amanda Witt. He was black, she was white, both so young and handsome, she thought, they should be ashamed of themselves. And they had a toddler too cute for words. Simply adorable. She had offered to look after the child if they ever needed a babysitter. She thought they had come to ask for her services. She looked forward to having a three-year-old around, even if it were only for a few hours.

"How are you two today?"

That was when she heard about the Atomic Church. In truth she had heard of it before. It had been all in the news when it first opened, and she remembered scoffing at the notion. A failed shopping center refurbished and rebuilt as a single mammoth church with just as mammoth a congregation. The "New City of God," their minister liked to call it.

"We'd love it if you came with us on Sunday. We think you'd enjoy it."

They were oh so nice, so gentle. She couldn't tell them that was not her sort of place.

Nothing could have prepared her for that odd gathering. More like a nation under one roof. Never in her sixty-two years had she been among so many human souls at once. The rumblings alone sounded like thunder. The main auditorium held ten thousand people, and was sandwiched between two vast wings containing, among other things, a nursery the size of a small school, a "worship gym" where one could work out while watching the sermon on jumbo monitors, four small theme chapels, several suites of administrative offices, a bookstore and record store, a gift shop, a café and a restaurant and a sandwich shop, an infirmary, and a children's recreation room that resembled Disneyland. The Atomic Church of God and Worship Center boasted a credit union, an employment agency, a marriage counseling service, and a culinary school ("learning to cook for Jesus!"). There were six choirs, four Christian rock bands—the Rolling Tongues of Fire, Loaves N' Phishes, the

Adam and Eve Project, Psalmsmack—and an inspirational rap group, Boyz 4 da Cross, that had a best-selling CD entitled *Gangbanging 4 da Lord*. There were four services on Sunday, and at least one major one every day, not to mention endless Bible studies and support groups, and a flotilla of outreach programs and lectures and encounter gatherings and forums that resembled activities aboard a luxury liner. In fact that's what the entire operation reminded her of: one vast ocean liner on land, afloat from the rest of the world. She would get through this service.

Then, after musical numbers and skits that made her think she was first at a rock concert, and then a Broadway play, and then a stadium-sized group therapy session, with the uproar and flash of a rock star-cum-head of state, onto center stage rushed the Atomic Reverend himself, Reverend Spike ("Are you ready to get nuclear for Jesus?"). Aside from having the physique of a professional wrestler and the good looks of a movie star, and a platinum tongue, the Reverend had a mystique that was bound up in his past. His father had been a famous African-American physicist, and his mother, part Japanese, part Hawaiian, a concert pianist. He had gone to excellent schools, and at a tender age made a fortune in computers, which he lost, and then another one with an Internet company, which was in turn wiped out like so much goofer dust. All before he was thirty. But did that stop Spike Eggleston? No, brothers and sisters. The Lord had an appointment for him stored in his great celestial PalmPilot. Hallelujah! The Lord told him to build him a city, a City of God, just as Saint Augustine had written about. And the Atomic Church was that city.

The standing applause took a while to die down, as the great tree trunk of a man strode back and forth across the immense stage, white teeth flashing, eyes manic with glee.

"Praise be to God, saints," he said as the crowd finally took their seats, though the mass of worshippers never quieted. Always there the hum and the occasional rally ejaculation of agreement, communication back and forth between the high-tech high priest and the pulsing Army of the Lord. The spectacle made Velmajean smile despite herself. This wasn't church, this was a movement.

"I'm happy this morning, saints. I've been talking to the CEO, the Chairman of the Board, the President of the Universe—hallelujah! And do you know what he told me?"

The response was akin to a thunderclap.

"That's right, children. Hallelujah! Our annual report's good. Our soul-stock is up! Our major asset—our Atomic faith in Christ Jesus our Lord—is through the roof! Hallelujah!" With that, balloons and confetti fell from the air like manna, and the response was seismic. The band struck up a disco version of "Soldiers of the Lord," and people not only leapt to their feet but danced, and for a time there was rejoicing in the aisles. Velmajean spied the frenzy the way a rabbit watches foxes frolic.

"Hug your brothers and sisters. Amen. Amen. Amen!" The Reverend led the worship pep rally for a good twenty minutes or more, before the lights dimmed, the stadium hushed, and the hulk from Honolulu settled down to his sermon, "God's 401(k) for You!" (which would be available at the next service on audiotape, videotape, CD, and DVD). By and by, somewhere in the midst of his message, long after the cute catchphrases had subsided, and the laser lights took a break, Velmajean found the Reverend downright moving. It was not his ocean-deep, river-smooth voice—the sort of voice that made you want to believe, to follow; after a spell it was hard to conceive that this voice did not know what it was talking about, did not come from another place; nor the fact that he was simply riveting to watch. But his words, tender, healing, inspiring, touched her. ("God's retirement plan is a Welcome Table of love, dearly beloved. The meek, the weak, the halt, the lame, the peacemakers and the sinners—hallelujah—will all be fed. Cleansed. Wrapped up in his bosom . . .") This, Velmajean thought, is how a sermon should make you feel.

At the end of the sermon Velmajean was on her feet along with the crowd crying "Hosea."

Make no mistake, Velmajean Swearington Hoyt was as levelheaded and as sensible as they come, not easily swayed by a good-looking man no matter how well he filled out a pair of jeans. Yes, she liked the Reverend, could listen to him all day, could watch him for the rest of her natural life. But it was not the Reverend's swell looks and sermon that convinced her in the end, that swept her along—it was the people. The overwhelming sense of fellowship, of belonging, of congregation in the truest sense: she felt as if she were becoming a member of a new nation, something fresh and wonderful, and she wanted to be a part of that new happening.

IN FACT she had been a member of the church for close to two years before she personally met the Reverend Spike. That occurred the day after the turkey barbecue incident.

He had actually been scheduled to be there that day—the

Annual Thanksgiving-in-May Celebration to feed the homeless at a strip mall in Durham—but on paper the Reverend Spike was always overbooked, double-booked, as if, one fine day, the Lord would see fit to actually split him into eight men to accomplish all the works necessary in his ministry.

Velmajean arrived at the parking lot early that day. There were to be fifteen other workers from the church to dispense the food. A poultry processing plant had donated turkeys galore, and the women and men in the Reach Out program had spent days roasting turkeys, frying turkeys, making turkey casseroles and turkey salads and turkey soup—gallons of turkey soup, as the chairperson reasoned, depending upon the turnout, the soup could be stretched (and ultimately frozen), yet remain filling and nutritious. Four fat gobblers had been left over. Velmajean volunteered to take them home to barbecue. She'd spent hours that night and the next morning slowly grilling the butterflied birds, deboning and hacking the meat into two large plastic tubs of delicious chopped barbecue with a strong vinegar-based sauce sure to please a crowd. Her wrists and forearms were still sore from the work. She had also stopped by on her way to pick up a gross of bread loaves donated by a local, upscale French bistro. Her car smelled of toasted sesame seeds, and new barbecue.

Thirty minutes before the appointed hour, a small group of men had gathered, smoking and milling about, talking loud. There was no sign of her fellow church members. Velmajean sat in the car, her mouth watering from the smells of piquant barbecue sauce, and the loaves of bread pungent even from the trunk. She listened to the all-news radio station.

She didn't get worried until fifteen minutes before the meal was to be served. The two vans with the Atomic Church of God and Worship Center logos were nowhere to be seen. A crowd of men and a smattering of women had gathered now. For the first time in many months, Velmajean regretted that she had not knuckled under and gotten a cell phone.

There came a knock to her window. There stood a young-ish man, chestnut brown, in a frayed-collar shirt and green fatigues. He had several days' growth of beard and his teeth were ivory snow white. He smiled at Velmajean as she rolled the window down.

"Miss, some of the guys were wondering if we got the wrong day for the Thanksgiving thing."

"No, no," Velmajean said. "It's supposed to be happening right now. I don't know where everybody is."

The man licked his lips. "Ummmm, that smells good. Barbecue?"

"Yeah, turkey barbecue. Made it myself."

The man paused and stared at Velmajean. To this day, of all the things that occurred that day, the look on that young man's face abided with her. Not a look so much of hunger, or of longing, or of weariness, though, to be sure, these powerful ingredients stewed there; but there understood, not pitied. Most powerfully there was a sense of a man clinging to his dignity, not to be melted for barbecue.

Later when asked what had moved her to get out of her car, take out the two tubs of barbecue, retrieve the 144 loaves of bread from the trunk, and begin, one by one, to serve the throng, she could only shrug and sigh. "It seemed like a good idea at the time."

She knew the real reason, but felt she could never find a

way to properly articulate it, to make anyone understand: she did not want that young man to have to ask.

Ninety-minutes later the two vans from the church arrived, heavy-laden with their cornucopia of turkey cuisine and condiments and Kool-Aid. They saw Velmajean Swearington Hoyt, alone and armed only with a spoon and a knife, cutting open loaf after loaf of bread, scooping up a decent amount of turkey barbecue, patiently feeding an entire tribe of men and women.

Perhaps that would have been the end of the matter, people might have spoken of the incident with warm hearts and glowing tones in that way one speaks of dedicated teachers, but she kept on and on and on. Despite the brothers and sisters hurriedly arranging the tables and turkey salad, turkey sandwiches, and now-tepid soup, for some odd reason the crowd gravitated around Velmajean, wanted to taste and be fed by the woman who had been serving them solo from the beginning. The loaves did not run out; the tub of barbecue never went empty. Each and every person in the crowd was filled.

A gentleman was quoted as saying: "That's some of the best barbecue I've ever tasted in my entire gall-durned life."

Later accounts put the number of people at over a thousand, which was unrealistic; the program had never served more than five hundred people at one time. Mrs. Frederica Stanforth and Mrs. Nellie Mae Washington both reckoned the crowd at more like a hundred and fifty to two hundred. But how the barbecued flesh of four turkeys and a big bag of bread could feed such a number escaped even their eagle eyes. Moreover: Velmajean never opened the second tub.

Velmajean understood that something had occurred but tried not to name it. She went home, tired, and fell into a cotton-candy sleep, gauzy, sweet, luscious, buoyed, and serene.

At first the rumors and talk percolated only among the Atomic saints, but, given the number of witnesses and the sheer size of the congregation, soon a new urban legend arose: a woman—her unfamiliar name, thankfully, had been lost in the retellings—had fed an entire crowd of men with a tub of barbecue and a basket of bread at the Quail Dale Square at Broad and Hollywood in Durham, North Carolina, a legend now being repeated all over the state. It was on Bingo Night that Velmajean first heard the word "miracle" applied to the incident. That was the first time Velmajean Swearington Hoyt began to feel, instead of blessed, afraid.

DEPENDING ON the scholar one asks, the Christ performed somewhere in the neighborhood of thirty-five miracles. By the time the Reverend had contacted Velmajean, inadvertently four more incidents had befallen her: dancing with her nephew on the pond at Abendigo Park; delivering a nonagenarian woman from Alzheimer's with a hug; touching the cheek of a young man who suffered from acute paranoid schizophrenia and watching him walk away smiling and whole of mind. She shook hands with a woman who suffered from carpal tunnel syndrome and the shooting pains vanished. By and by, her name had been divulged and crowds appeared along Piney View Lane. The doorbell rang constantly. After six people—a blind man, a woman with kidney failure, a deaf boy, a quadriplegic man, a woman with breast cancer, and another with multiple sclerosis—had been cured, her neighbors declared they had had enough, and put a stop to the steady stream with a barrage of calls to the police department and the sheriff. By that point Velmajean had already become more and more disturbed. People turned up asking her to pay their Visa bills, to cure them of sexual addictions, to provide winning lotto numbers and to palliate penile dysfunction. When she heard the sirens and the official barking on electrified megaphones, she felt two things: relief and a shame, more than she would care to admit. To be sure, there was a great joy, a deep, exhilarating sense of awe at the works being performed through her—not once did she take responsibility for the changes—but with each new face, with each new plea, she had experienced a creeping sadness and confusion. "I'm looking for a miracle," the song went. For as long as she could remember, Velmajean believed she believed in miracles. Small and large. Mysterious and home-grown. She believed angels walked among us. She believed that folks were inexplicably healed of dread ills. That prayers were answered. Only now the purpose of miracles among men was less clear to her. Were they to demonstrate God's love, the power of faith? Or to do good? Was one better than the other? Was it more important to have faith than to be made whole? She had not reckoned on the differing views— if indeed there was a difference. And frankly, the contemplation made her head hurt.

The police and state troopers set up barricades and stood guard, and Velmajean was left to worry and fret. Part of her, roaming about the empty house, vacuuming, dusting, defrosting the freezer, was secretly terrified, though she did her best to hide it from herself. Theretofore she had been successful in not asking questions about what was happening to her. But no longer: Why me? What have I been chosen to do? What have I done to deserve this? That night she did not sleep well at all. Her dreams were beyond baffling: she dreamt of being in a choir of gorgeous, multicolored, naked angels, singing hip-hop songs in a language she did not understand; she dreamt of frantically trying to finish a supper for Jesus and a party of twelve who were going to arrive at any minute, and the damn turkey was raw; she dreamt she was watching television with a roomful of long-dead people—her mother, her father, her cousin Agnes among them—but everyone ignored her and left her to watch 60 *Minutes* by herself. She missed her husband as if he had died the day before.

Demonstrating that he was well brought up, the Reverend Spike had the good manners to call first. Overwhelmed by calls, Velmajean had broken down and purchased an answering machine, so she was lucky to pick up his call.

She served him tea on her sun porch and was bemused and delighted by her pastor, the pastor, curiously enough, who had paid her no attention in the twenty-four months since she had joined his behemoth church.

"You aren't getting bored in this big house all by yourself, are you?"

"No more than usual, Reverend. And I have all these nice men you sent to watch over me to play pinochle with at night. Not for money, of course."

They chitted and chatted. Velmajean found it difficult to put her finger on what made this gigantic figure so attractive ("More tea, Reverend?"), not merely the composition of his face, the symmetry, the rich salmon complexion, the intimidatingly white and well-formed teeth, the ink-black eyes ("Thank you, sister"). No, it was the way he insinuated himself upon the individual you ("Did I ever show you pictures of the new baby?"), the self-possession, the self-power, the self-projection of self into yourself ("Isn't he a little cherub? Look at that"), the way yourself was locked into himself when he spoke with you—it was a presence that told you: *Don't worry. You're with me.*

"Tell me about your husband," he asked, holding a framed portrait of Parker.

"Oh, I think he would have liked you, Reverend, and you him."

They spent a time talking about her family, the old township, her years alone. He told her charming stories about his own family, and meeting the president. They prayed together. When they were done, the Reverend Spike Eggleston became a little more businesslike. "I was wondering, Sister Velma, if you would feel more . . . well, secure. More comfortable in a hotel. You know, we have nice guest suites down at the church. You might—"

But Velmajean demurred. She felt better at home. "Honestly, Reverend, I don't know what I'd do if I didn't have a floor to mop or some dusting to do. Keeps me in my right mind, if you know what I mean."

"Okay. For now, Mrs. Hoyt. I understand completely. But you might start thinking . . . There may come a time when you absolutely have to be in more secure quarters." With her permission, he had enlisted members of the church and a professional security team to guard her home. He could not stress enough, he told her—her hand resting in his palm—how much he was concerned about her safety.

With finesse, he pulled from his leather valise a sheaf of impeccably typed pages—itineraries, schedules, flowcharts, contracts—and he told her about the Plan. It was a dizzying outline of the church's, i.e., the Reverend Spike Eggleston's, plan to help Velmajean Swearington Hoyt "manage" her miracles. There was talk of power of attorney, profit sharing ("with the church, of course"), of media deals and S corporations. "I'm certain, Sister Velma, that this is the Lord's plan for you. To show that his power is here among us. And we must act quickly. The telecast is already scheduled for next Sunday."

"Telecast?"

"Yes, both network and cable."

"I know I shouldn't ask this question—shouldn't ask it ever—but do you have any idea why me?"

"The Lord works in mysterious ways, his wonders to behold."

Velmajean simply fixed him with a cold stare, more than a little weariness knit across her brow.

To his credit the Reverend cast his eyes down and sighed, as if to acknowledge the fact that Velmajean Swearington Hoyt was in no mood for easy biblical quotations. "Sister Velma, I have no idea. Maybe a reward. Maybe a curse. Maybe it will be revealed to you, to us, one day. Maybe it will go down as another of his mysterious manifestations. Another episode of *Unsolved Mysteries*."

He gave her that underwear-catalog smile, and she felt better. Not due to the charisma, but to his seeming honesty. She felt a smidgen less alone.

———

THE DAY didn't approach quickly. It seemed now she was a prisoner in her own home, which was at least now spotless. There was no doubt in her mind that the Reverend Spike had her best interests at heart, and was about God's work. A panel of doctors and scientists and skeptics had been invited to examine the infirm in advance, and to testify to the global public afterward as to their states, followed by the laying on of hands, and the reevaluation of their situations.

"And what if the Lord is offended and decides not to heal them?"

"I have faith he will, Sister Velma."

Was it better to quietly work miracles, to heal the sick, fix the wrongs of the world? Or lead the masses to the Holy of Holies? That was the debate roiling through the late-night radio talk shows and Internet chat rooms and cable programs. No doubt it was in the mind of the Deacon Wilford Brown, late of St. Thomas Baptist Church, when he came to call.

Dusk had just inked the air when one of the bodyguards told Mrs. Hoyt there was an elderly gentleman out front who said he was an old friend and insisted he had to see her.

He was in a wheelchair and rolled by his niece, Hettie, whom he had called from the bed of his nursing home in Raleigh, telling her she had to take him to see the woman he had known from the cradle.

Wilford Brown was now eighty-seven and had lost a leg to sugar diabetes. Velmajean had known him all her life, and for as long as she could remember, he had been chairman of the deacon board of their now-erstwhile congregation.

"Sister, girl," he greeted her with wide-open arms. He felt

frail in her arms, all his life a tall, sturdy, bullish mechanic of a man. His fingers were still sausage-thick, though she could never remember them being so immaculately clean.

Over decaf he inquired about her family and her health, while his niece watched TV. He seemed loath to jump right into the business that had brought him to Piney View Lane, Velmajean could see. But could it be more obvious?

"I'm a little worried about you, baby girl. Looks like you got ahold of something—or something's got ahold of you one—and it's running away with you. Is all this talk true?"

"I can imagine you've heard a bunch of mess, but a lot of what they say is true."

"That little girl? The one in the car crash?"

Velmajean nodded.

"The barbecue?"

Again she nodded yes.

The old gent took a long silence, rubbed his face, and looked away. Velmajean felt more than a bit uncomfortable. Requests always made her feel uncomfortable.

But what he said next took her off guard: "And what do you reckon old Reverend Barden back home would say about all this foolishness?"

"Foolishness?"

"Oh, come on, Velmajean. All this mess with the TV, and that jack-legged, wrassler-looking, no-good, lying, car salesman of a preacher got his claws all up in this. What do you think I'm talking about, baby girl? I've known you all your born days, and the Lord knows I figured you to have more sense than to let yourself be *used* like this."

"If anybody's using me, I'll tell you: it ain't Reverend Spike."

"Listen at you. 'Reverend Spike.' Is you blind?"

"The Reverend might be . . . unconventional, but he's sincere. I know it in my heart. He's for real. I really do believe that."

Wilford snorted. "'Unconventional.'" It was as if the word were a sour taste on his tongue.

The crash through the window was not what Velmajean would remember. She heard the glass sunder and tinkle on the floor, the wood split and crack and splinter as the body hurtled through her kitchen door. But the way Mr. Wilford first jumped, and then tried to get out of his wheelchair, and the look upon his face when he realized he was trapped, made her want to cry. Velmajean did not scream, but the deacon's niece did—how did she get to the kitchen so quickly?

The man was wearing the same black overcoat, now slightly torn, though it was his face, sans sunglasses, that she fixed upon. Where before he had a kindly visage, he now seemed to be frothing and his bloodshot eyes leered. He smelled awful, like spoiled milk mixed with overcooked cabbage. In fact Velmajean soon realized he was wearing the same suit as well, now torn, leaf- and straw-mottled.

Mr. Wilford hollered at first. Then said, "Get," as if he were shooing away a puppy.

The knife sliced through the air, not with a singing sound, but with a bat wing's flap. Twice he swung at Velmajean, who just stood there, at first, afraid to leave Mr. Wilford, and fighting the overwhelming need to pee, and pee bad.

The other thing that surprised her was the sound the gun made. Nothing like the loud bang she had heard at the movies or on TV. More a pop, like a firecracker. On the floor, the stranger convulsed and held his wounded shoulder, the blood—prune-juice dark—fanning out caterpillar-speed onto her yellow tiles.

The security guard told her to stay away, but it seemed so patently, so lightbulb-clear, what she had to do. As she bent over him, her hand moving toward the bleeding spot, her former African chief, her fantasy Secret Service agent, stared at her and mouthed: "Who said . . . Who said . . . who said . . ."

"What? What are you saying?"

"Who said it was from God?"

ENDING #2: [from *The Book of Velmajean Hoyt*]

Wilford's niece's high piercing scream seemed to go on forever—how did she get to the kitchen so fast? Velmajean had only seen the knife flash, once, twice. And then he stood still, staring at her. That pain was on the outside, as if she had received a long paper cut on her belly. On the inside was only a dim pressure, and a throbbing, and then a pouring. In some dull, still-functioning, stubborn place inside her brain, she understood in a crystalline way that she was in shock. She had taken a course on emergency medicine, years ago, back when she was an office manager. And she had to pee, and pee bad.

He stood there staring at her, and she wondered why she had ever judged him as being beautiful. His jet lips, now parched, ashy, and cracked, moved, but it was only after the pop of the security guard's gun brought him to his knees that she finally made out what he had said to her: "Who said it was from God?"

ENDING #3: [from *The Pentecost of VSH*]

The security guards—the paid one, Fletcher Cross, a fat white man with cherry cheeks, and a young man from church, Buzz Terrington, bear-big and the color of a fine leather jacket, and with a penchant for video games—tackled the intruder simultaneously. Velmajean soon turned away. Mr. Wilford's niece had wheeled him from the kitchen as he called out to Velmajean in confusion and fear. "Are you okay? Velmajean? Velma?"

After wrecking the dinner table, two chairs, the coffeemaker—the glass carafe simply exploded—and the cabinet door under the sink crashed in, the two men subdued the smelly man.

His face bloody, tears wetting his face, he snarled and struggled to get away. It was not at all clear to Velmajean that these two men could hold him down.

"Call the police!" Buzz said. "911!"

"I already did," Mr. Wilford's niece said from the doorway. "They'll be here any minute. Hold him!"

Velmajean took a step forward, trying to see the man's face clearly, to understand. He fixed her face with a glare so intense it almost made her cry. He spit at her, making her jump back.

"Who said it was from God?" he hollered. "Who told you that lie?"

ENDING #4: [from *The Gospel of Velmajean Swearington Hoyt*]

Mr. Wilford snorted. "'Unconventional.'" It was as if the word were a sour taste on his tongue.

Later Velmajean would remember the sound of the gun firing to be more like the pop of a firecracker.

"What the hell?" Mr. Wilford began rolling his chair toward the back door, toward the pop.

Apparently the guards had warned the man. They would later tell the police they had called to him as he ran toward the house, but he would not stop. Fletcher Cross, licensed to carry a gun, fired only once.

Now the floodlights were on, and in the middle of Velmajean's deck lay writhing her Secret Service agent, her black angel-helper, her once-vision, now nowhere near angelic: he wore the same thick coat, the same suit, tattered now, smelling like rotten cabbage and piss. Buzz Terrington held him down, but he gave little resistance, instead growling like a wild animal. "Shut up," Buzz yelled. "Keep still. An ambulance is on the way, you dumb shit." Velmajean could smell the fear on the other two guards, who had come round to watch.

The man had been shot in the shoulder, and was clutching it with his right hand. The hand was wet with blood, and between grimaces and snarls, the strange man sucked air as if it were hard to breathe. Heedless of any potential danger, in fact convinced of some plan, divine or otherwise, Velmajean made her way to the fallen trespasser.

"Don't touch me!" The man's words were distinct, clear and loud. "Don't you come near me, you whore."

"Wha—"

"I know who you are." The man winced, but tried to slide back from Velmajean. He began to cry. "It was not meant to be like this."

Now Why Come That Is?

That squall. That squall: metallic and beastly, squalling, coming from the bottom of hell itself, a squall full of suffering and pleas for mercy, a squall so familiar since Percy's earliest days, from when he was a little boy feeding his daddy Malcolm's Poland China brood sows . . .

But he didn't want to hear it now, damnit, not now, no, for now Percy Terrell was deep inside a dream. He and Elvis were on the town—was it Memphis? New Orleans? Nashville?—he didn't really know, and it didn't really matter. 'Cause he was in this diner with the King after a wild night of drinking and pool—the velvet night as tangible as the sheets in which he entangled himself at this moment of the dream—at this moment when he and Elvis sat in the diner with the checkered red-and-white tablecloth with two blondes, one each, one for him and one for the King; and Percy had his hand on the milky-red thigh of that big-legged gal who smiled through her smacking gum and that leg was so soft and so inviting and she smiled even bigger as Percy moved his hands up that thigh toward—

But that squalling got louder as if someone were murdering that damn hog over and over, calling Percy back to wakefulness, and Percy didn't want to wake up, not with this fine big-legged thing sitting next to him, practically begging for it, and Elvis looking on across the table through his sunglasses, his arm around his sweetie for the night.

What's your name again, hon?

Evangeline, she said.

Evangeline. What a pretty name. Yeah. Percy slid his hand a little higher. Yeah. What's that smell?

At that moment, the moment when the dreamer begins to lose the threads and fabric of his dream, Percy began to dwell more and more on that vile, that powerful and obnoxious odor. Was it the woman? No, hadn't smelled her before. She looked clean enough. And the squalling kept on and on and the smell of hog. Hog. *Hog.*

Percy sat up in the bed, wide awake. As he blinked and focused, the squalling continued, but not in the bedroom now, and presently stopped altogether. Percy swung his feet over the side of the bed and one foot landed in something warm and slick, the sensation at once comforting and sickening, ooey and gooey and warm. His bare foot slid on the Carolina-blue carpet.

"Shit."

Shit. There it was, and Percy's heart almost leapt for joy. Almost. His foot was in a turd. But he had proof. At long last the evidence he needed.

"Rose," he called to his snoring wife, turning on the bedside lamp. "Rose"—he began to shake her. "Rose, wake up. Look, honey, look. That damn bastard has been here and he's left his calling card. Wake *up!*"

Rose Terrell smacked her mouth absently, and frowned, the sleep so deep around her eyes. "Hmmm?"

"Look, honey, look." Percy held his soiled foot perilously close to his wife's face. "See, Rose, see it there! I won't lying. He was here. That bastard was here." Rose opened one eye, moved it from her husband's brown-stained foot to his gleeful face, she closed it and turned over. "Percy? Take a bath. You stink." Rose brought the sheet over her head, and almost as quickly began to snore.

Percy, a little dejected, removed his foot, and with a little hesitation began to wipe it clean with a tissue. Yet he was not completely deflated, no. He was not crazy, as his besoiled foot and annoyed nostrils bore witness. This proof was what he had needed, he had finally gotten a physical sign, a residue; and with all the stubbornness his Scots-Irish blood could muster, he was going to prove, at least to himself, that he was not mad: he was indeed being visited by a hog.

A reddish-brown rusty razorback, to be exact, an old boar hog with unpulled incisors long enough to be called tusks, kite-big, floppy ears, and massive testicles the size of a catcher's mitt. For now on six weeks this hog would appear out of nowhere, without warning or preamble, anywhere—in the living room, in the cab of his pickup, at the store, entreating Percy, staring at Percy, following Percy, and the damned fool thing of it was that nobody but Percy had—could—see it; and Percy had no idea how it came and went. Rose Terrell had listened to Percy—who for not one minute believed the hog to be a figment of his imagination—and was absolutely unconvinced. In fact, seeing that Percy otherwise had all his faculties, she clearly just assumed Percy was fooling again— like the time he swore up and down that there was a snake in the plumbing (a very bad joke)—and just ignored him. Percy could tell that was what she had figured, and had given up on her, had simply stopped commenting on the hog, even when it showed up and sat at his side all through breakfast. And now he was assured the whole thing might be a practical joke being played on him. But by who? He wasn't certain. But he'd find out in time. Got your hog right here, mister. So Percy would play along, 'cause there was no way in hell she and everybody else didn't see that damned hog.

But now, now he had evidence and substance. Now he knew the whole damn thing could be explained away. Something someone else could see, smell, hell, even taste. And though, upon reflection, he had no idea what to do next, other than clean up the mess, sitting there on the side of the bed, his foot encrusted with drying excrescence, Percy Terrell felt a glimmer of something like hope, a sense that perhaps he was not going mad.

That first night he had seen it, madness was far from his mind, the whole occurrence had simply been a matter of negligence, of chance, of curious curiosity. He had been at his desk around eight o'clock in his office at the back of the general store, deep in thought, poring over tax document after tax document, trying desperately to find a mistake his fool accountant had made, cussing at this damn new machine Rose bought him, damn thing was supposed to be fast, digital and all, but it kept losing the figures, coming up with zero or *e*, and . . .

Percy had heard something outside his office, in the belly of the store, something clicking on the old hardwood floor. He stopped, tilted his head to give a listen. A few more clicks. "Rose? That you?" He didn't hear the clicks. "Malcolm? Percival? Philip?" Nothing, just the refrigerator cycling off, a car passing by outside, the buzz of the overhead light. Percy went back to work. Presently he heard it again, but closer, decidedly a "click" or a "clock" or a "cluck" sound, of something hard, yet a bit muffled against the wood. Something walking. Percy got up to inspect. Everything looked shadow-drenched and shadow-full, the ghostly beams of the emergency lights enhancing the shadowscape, making the rows of fishing rods and gun racks and boxes of mufflers and barrels of three-penny nails and the yarn section, the gumball machine, the pipes and monkey wrenches and shovels and baby dolls, seem about to move. Yet all was bathed in after-closing quiet, and still. Percy saw this dim world every night and he had never given it a second thought: same as it was during the day. But for some reason, this night, at this moment, it felt a little spooky.

"Who that out there?" Nothing. "Store's closed, now." By and by, Percy began to feel silly, just a tree branch knocking against the roof, and turned around and set his mind to line 27e on page 12 of whatever the hell that form was. After a bit his mind was once again stinging with the unshakable accuracy of what his accountant had ciphered true, and how much he would not be putting in T-bills this year, when he felt a presence. Someone was standing at the door. He didn't want to give in to the surprise, and his mind instantly went to the three rifles on the wall behind him, just below the flattened rattlesnake skin he had tanned himself. If they had a gun trained on him, he wouldn't be able to reach it in time. Reluctantly he looked up.

Percy actually hollered. And flung his chair back so hard that the wall shook and the bronze gubernatorial citation he had received in 1975 fell to the ground with a clank. Had it been a human-being person, Percy would have been ready, but before him stood this great big ole hog, its head jerking here and there, inspecting the place, coming back every now and again to Percy, its eyes piercing and unhumanly human.

"Git!" Percy said from the chair, collecting himself, wondering how the hell a hog got in his store. "Git on, now, git." Percy sprang to his feet, now simply annoyed, annoyed that someone had obviously left the door open or it had come open and this hog got in. He grabbed a broom from behind the door and waved it at the hog, no stranger to the dumb, docile nature of the creatures. "Git on, now. Git on." Wondering who it could belong to, hoping it hadn't shit in the store. Damn. Damn. Damn. The hog grunted and began to back up. In his frustration Percy hit the creature on the nose with the broom. "Git on out of here and back to where you belong!"

With that crack of the broom, the hog backed up two steps and raised its head, opening its swine mouth wide, and let out a bracing, brassy bellow, a bellow of outrage and anger, loud enough to make Percy step back and almost drop the broom. And with a quickness that belied its enormous size, the hog leapt and ran, the clackety-clackety of its hoofy gallop reporting against the store's walls. Percy chased after it, but soon realized he didn't hear the hog anymore. He switched on the store lights, which momentarily rendered him blind with their glare. He didn't see the hog. He searched up and down each aisle, calling to it, stopping to listen, but heard nothing. After about twenty minutes, his frustration at the boil, he got on the horn and called his sons and wife and the two men who worked in the store. "No, Dad. I don't know nothing about no hog." "Percy, I locked and checked all the doors fore I left. How could a hog get in there?" "'Swhat I want to know, Ed!" When his youngest and dimmest son, Philip Malcolm, suggested, "Well, maybe he climbed in through the window," Percy just slammed the phone down, annoyed, angered, pissed off beyond anything he could remember in recent memory. He sat at his desk, stomped his foot once, sighed, crammed all the tax forms and files into his satchel, turned out the lights, and left.

Days passed and the memory of the mystery hog began to bore Percy with the equality of its nagging and its curiosity. He went about his days with the grim joylessness and banal glory with which he filled each day. Rising at five to feed the dogs, watching the farm reports from Greenville, eating breakfast that Rose prepared herself since Agnes didn't arrive until eight; going to open the store, checking everything; driving around the farm, checking this, checking maybe having a meeting in Crosstown with his lawyer or his banker or the manager of the mill, lunch most days at Nellie's Cafe, a plate of barbecue that his doctor said he should at least cut back on, with a glass of ice tea—these were his days, as empty as they were full. And even Percy, Lord of York County, had dreams of going off away somewhere, maybe to go on safari, hunting big game. He had done that once, back in '52, and had a fairly good time in Kenya, got a good shot off at an antelope, but didn't bag a thing. These days it was too much trouble, especially since those bleeding hearts and tree huggers made it illegal. He'd met a man a few years back who said that they'd guarantee a big kill in one of those African countries, Percy forgot which one, but it would cost him somewhere in the neighborhood of fifty thousand American dollars, the man had said, and Percy had said, Thank you kindly, and goodbye, 'cause Malcolm Terrell didn't raise no fool. No sir. Thank you sir. So he figured he'd content himself with deer and coon and ducks and the occasional big fish, though, truth to tell, at fifty-eight, Percy Terrell was losing his taste for killing things, something he'd never admit to another soul. Some days just being in the woods of an autumn or in a boat under the big sky was reward in and of itself. Perhaps Percy was at a point that he could even admit it to himself.

A week and six days passed, and Percy had damn near forgotten about the hog—he remembered really, mostly, that feeling of horror that had involuntarily gripped him upon the sight of the thing. That afternoon he stopped by one of the twenty-tree turkey houses he owned, a set of five over in Mill Swamp, where Ab Batts was fixing the feeding system that had been breaking with annoying frequency. This turkey house was about thirty yards long and Percy could see Ab bent over at work at the far end. Percy despised these dumb creatures, gobbling and gibbering about his feet and ankles, their heads just above knee level, the sight of their red and gelatinous wattles making him sometimes shiver with disgust. Turkeys were too dumb to walk out of the rain, but sometimes one would get its feathers riled and would peck at you. One turkey rooster made him so mad once that he stomped it to death before Percy realized what he was doing, which he later regretted 'cause the price went up that very day.

As Percy waded through the dirty white mess of jabbering poultry, kicking and shooing, he called out to Ab, and

Ab waved at him and went on working. As Percy got about halfway into the house, the turkeys started making more and more of a commotion, and started parting even before Percy got in their midst, bunching along the wire-mesh walls, hollering, crying even, it seemed to Percy's ears. Percy looked about, baffled, and even Ab Batts jerked up, amazed at the unruly fuss. Then Ab's eyes fixed on Percy with a mild degree of consternation and puzzlement, but Percy came to see it was not him Ab had transfixed in his glare.

"Boss," yelled Ab, "what you bring a hog in here for?"

Astonished and confounded, Percy stared at Ab, trying to make sure he understood what he was saying, and, as he said, "Wha . . ." he looked round about him, and directly behind him stood that same damned hog, sniffing at the turkeys, whose racket was at this point of an earsplitting quality. And ever so briefly, in the middle of this feather frenzy, this poultry pandemonium, ever so momentarily, eye-to-eye with this porcine beast, this stalking ham, Percy felt that he was not in Tims Creek, North Carolina; that he was not Percival Malcolm Terrell, first and only son of Malcolm Terrell; not chairman and chief executive officer of the Terrell Corporation, county commissioner, and deacon—he was a mere blip on some otherness, some twisted reality. He didn't know where he was.

Ab rushed after the hog and, after some effort, chased it from the turkey house. "'Tweren't your hog, I reckon," Ab laughed off the situation, walking up to Percy, who had not really moved.

"Ah . . . no." Percy rubbed his eyes, not wanting to betray himself to Ab. "No, don't know where it came from. Musta just followed me in here. Didn't even see it. Ain't that something?"

"Musta been one of Joe Richards's. He been catching the devil with his hogs. Got one of them newfanged, fancy-dancy hog operations, over there he has, and can't keep 'em from getting out." A predicament that Ab clearly found amusing, as he laughed some more.

Somehow, hearing Ab speak of the hog as a piece of a machine, a cog, an it, something that belonged to someone, and eventually on a plate, reassured Percy and filled in that momentary sense of a void; made him, oddly enough, whole again in his mind.

But that would be the last time he would feel that way for many a day, for, two days later, the hog appeared in the back of his pickup truck while he was driving back to Tims Creek from Crosstown. He stopped the truck and got out, worrying that the hog might vanish and convince him that he was more than a little touched. But the hog remained standing there in the bed of the truck, and Percy reached down and patted it, saying, "Whose hog are you, fella?" feeling its warm, rough, hairy flanks flinch beneath his hand, the coarseness and the solid meat. Percy laughed out loud and shook his head and drove on to Tims Creek. He stopped at McTarr's Convenience Store in the middle of town and got out, seeing within the store Joe Batts and Tom McShane and Teddy Miller and Woodrow Johnson, standing around the microwave counter. "Hey, y'all," Percy said upon entering. "Anybody lost a hog?"

The men looked one to another, and all around out the window, searching with their eyes.

Woodrow took a swig of his Pepsi. "Where you see a hog, captain?"

"Out in my truck is where. Anybody heard anything about somebody losing one?"

Everyone went out to inspect the now-empty truck.

"All right, now. Who took the hog out that truck?"

The men, smiling, a bit confused, watched one another, a little uneasy now.

Percy looked to see if anyone else was about. He noted a young woman filling up her compact Japanese-made piece a mess. "Hey there. You seen anybody take a hog out this here flatbed?"

The teenager shrugged and said, "I ain't seen nothing and nobody. There won't nothing in that truck to begin with."

"There was!" Percy turned to the men, who were no longer looking him in the eye. He walked to the side of the store. Nothing. Just a lone tractor.

"All right, now." He came back before the men, who dared not look him in the face. "Where is it? There was a goddamned boar hog in this goddamned truck and I want to know which sonofabitch put it—took it—"

"Percy? You all—"

"Yes, I'm all right, goddamnit, and when I find out who—" Percy heard himself, heard himself yelling, heard how ridiculous he was sounding, him, Percy Terrell, before these men who respected and admired him, men who he knew secretly all hated and dreaded him as well. And he caught himself, the way a snake handler catches the head of an angry snake; caught himself mid-roar, and started laughing, just like that, laughing, started exerting control of the situation and of himself. He winked, "Had you going, didn't I," and strolled past the men, who were not laughing, yet, who followed him into the store, where Percy went over to the drink cooler and hauled out a Pepsi and drank deeply, saying, "So, Tom, did you ever find that foaling mare the other night?"

Still a bit uneasy, Tom McShane sat down, clearly a mite rattled, and said: "Ah, yeah, Percy, yeah I did, but it was too late, they both died. Hated to lose that mare and that colt. 'Twas a colt, you know."

The men fell into commiserating and talking about this and that, and the queer spell Percy had cast over the meeting diminished by and by, though the specter of his curious behavior clung to the air like a visible question mark. And Percy, who was oh so loath to admit it to himself, knew that he had no idea what the hell was going on; knew that in some inescapable way he was, at bottom, more than a little afraid.

The visitations stepped up after that in frequency and in their curious and unexpected nature. The hog would appear of its own accord now in the house—once when he was shaving he saw it in the mirror; once when he and Rose were in the living room watching a World War II documentary on cable ("Rose?" "Yes, Percy," she said, not looking up from her needlepoint. "Nothing." And the hog got up, during a commercial, walked out of the room, and didn't return that night)—now in town—once in a meeting at the mill with John Buzkoswski, the general manager, the hog walked from behind the manager's desk, with him sitting at it, and the manager saw nothing and Percy had to pretend he saw nothing; and once while attending a court proceeding over a bankrupt furniture store he owned a percentage in, Percy swore he saw the hog walk across the front of the room and expected someone to say something, anything, to acknowledge the animal. But no one said a word, not even Percy.

Every day now, the hog was sure to show, and everywhere that Percy went the hog was sure to go. He had given up asking if anyone else had seen it. He was even no longer certain that it was an elaborate practical joke that everyone was playing on him, a joke that would suddenly come to a crescendo, a punch line, and that everyone in the whole blessed county would have an enormous, gut-wrenching, wont-that-funny-as-hell laugh over, and then Percy would come out looking the good sport and the business would be finished. But nothing of the sort occurred. So Percy waited, for days and days, and he became a little resigned to his swinish companion, and had even commenced to talking to it on occasion, when they were alone, sometimes in the cab of his truck, where it would sit, as tame as any dog. And, on these queer occasions, Percy would think how sanely insane it all was, and that he himself might be, without a doubt, crazy. But one stubborn and nagging fact remained: Ab had seen it. And as long as he didn't remark upon the creature, Percy's life was going along swimmingly. However, one day his bafflement reached a new level of strangeness. He had gone over to his son Malcolm II's house, where his daughter-in-law was bad off with the flu. Rose, who was frantic with preparing and planning for a church trip to the Holy Land next month, asked Percy to take some food Agnes had prepared over to poor ailing Maria. Malcolm and Maria Terrell had five children, three boys, Percival, Malcolm III, and Richard (after Maria's father), and two girls, Rose and Electra, and Percy felt awful proud of his progeny, especially the second boy, who bore not only his father's name but his father's likeness, but with a sweetness his great-grandfather had never possessed. That day, as he blew the truck horn, the children all ran out the front door to greet Granddaddy Percy, and he got out of the truck and reached into his coat pockets for the treats he never forgot to bring for them—much to the disquiet of their mother, who had the unfortunate lapse of good judgment to tell him to his face that she disapproved of giving candy to her children, whereupon her husband Malcolm himself made it clear that you don't object to Percy Terrell's largesse, and besides a little candy won't hurt 'em none, and so she now just grinned and beared it, the way Percy felt she should have from the beginning—but this day the children inexplicably ran to the other side of the truck. Percy walked around to discover them cooing and cuddling with the hog. Little Malcolm III clambered onto its broad back, and, to Percy's amazement, rode the hog like a miniature pachyderm.

Percy stood there with a feeling like bliss and quiet resolve. "Y'all see that ole hog, do you?"

Rose, age eight, looked up as if to say, *What kind of question is that?* "Where'd you get him, Granddaddy? He's *big*!"

Percy lit a cigarette and watched the innocent gallivanting for the duration of his smoke, a guilty pleasure he had promised the doctor he'd quit, while promising himself he'd just cut back; he watched with a feeling of warmth at the sight of his issue's issue having fun, a feeling that he rarely felt, a feeling that he actually felt uncomfortable feeling, yet felt good feeling. Over it all, in the middle of it all, under it all, was the strange stalking porker, whose presence, for a few moments, he actually accepted, accepted as a queer reality, and at the moment, even enjoyed.

Presently, Percy took the food in to Maria, who, from her bed, asked what the children were doing out there, and Percy almost said, *Oh, they're just playing with my hog*, the reality behind the word "my" pricking his brain as he thought it, suddenly aware of the connotations, the meaning of the word "my." My hog. "They're just playing."

After sitting for a few minutes with the mother of the children who would carry on his family name, his name, Percy kissed her upon the brow and ordered her to get better—she was a good-looking woman, even when she was under the weather—and returned to the playing children, now three of whom were perched on the back of the patient, ever-suffering, ever-enormous hog. Percy gently lifted his grandchildren off its back, one by one, and slapped its rump. "Go on, now. Git on." The hog didn't move. "Go on now, go on back to where you belong." Percy kicked it.

"Granddaddy! Don't!"

"Quiet now, honey. This ain't my hog. 'Sgot to go on back to where it came from."

"But Granddaddy . . ."

The hog turned around and looked at Percy with something that Percy felt to be an accusation. Without further ado or prodding, the hog trotted off in the direction of the house. Richard started to run after it, but Percy made him come back. "Leave him go, boy. Leave him go."

That night the hog left its aromatic calling card.

Having exhausted every avenue he could consciously consider short of going to a doctor—or a vet—Percy took what, for him, was a bold and unexpected step: he went to visit Tabitha McElwaine.

All the colored folks who worked for him swore up and down about Miss Tabitha, who was known throughout five counties as the best midwife and rootworker around. They mentioned her name with reverence and a touch of awe: "Went to see Miss Tabitha 'bout it." As if, Percy contemplated with scorn, she was the Lord Jesus Christ Him Damn Self. When they spoke to him of her, he called them damn fools to their faces, saying they'd be better off just burning their money. "But Mr. Percy, you just don't know." "I know damn well enough that that old fool can't do nothing but make piss and deliver babies, and God can take care of that without her around!" But the colored swore by her and gave her money left and right to cure ailments and make somebody fall in love with them; to make them prosperous and to take out revenge, happily handing over hard-earned currency to that lying heifer. And if he discovered a white person doing such a thing, Percy would refuse to speak to them for years on end.

The old witch, who was about the same age as Malcolm, Percy's father, lived alone in the old McElwaine mansion that proudly stood in what was left of her granddaddy's 208-acre spread, purchased after the Civil War. Now only five acres remained, the balance now belonging to the Terrell family, as Percy's own father had seen to. Legend had it that Malcolm's daddy had killed her daddy over it, and the black folk had in turn murdered Malcolm. But nobody could prove anything, and Percy kept the land, and they kept their hatred.

Percy stood there now, at the front door of the old Federal-style house, improbable in its competence and simple grandeur, well kept up, recently painted, red brick and white trim, fearfully large crape myrtle bushes ringing the yard, and Percy wondered how an ex-slave could have possibly built it alone, thinking the story to be a lie in the first place. As he stood there Percy dared not admit to himself how desperate he had to be to come to this lowliness, how perplexed and damned, and, at base, simply bored by this intrusion, this haunting; how his otherwise simple and orderly life had been thrown into chaos, and how he, Percy Terrell, was at his wit's end. How he wanted an old black woman to tell him, an old white man, what he must do to release himself. But at that time, though he knew this all to be true, he would not allow the thoughts to form in his noggin, he just moved forward with an inexorable logic, and a bitter will for exorcism. So he told himself nothing, as he stood there knocking, knocking, repeatedly, annoyed and calling out, finding the door to be open, and just inviting himself on in.

Grudgingly impressed again, he marveled at how finely wrought and finely attended the house's interior had been, how cavernous its halls and rooms seemed—larger than the ones at his house—fixed up like a New Orleans cathouse with lace and doilies over the velvet-upholstered chairs, and with ferns and potted plants aplenty, gossamer curtains, and daguerreotypes of some solemn-looking Negroes staring down at him from the walls.

Without prologue he saw her straightaway, on the other side of a big room, through yet another between them, standing by a big and dark stone fireplace. She stood there, still a tall and slim woman, her head now white with gray, a red shawl over her shoulders, wearing a long blue dress that looked modern and fine, as if she'd just ordered it out of a Spiegel catalog. Percy walked down the carpet toward her.

"Nice hog," she said, not cracking a smile or moving a muscle.

"Um," Percy grunted, not wanting to acknowledge his co-visitor, walking by his side, his head febrile with the fact of his being there, in her damn house, fighting with the inevitable fact of humility, of asking, of a need he for once could not solve with a credit card or the writing of a check.

He came within a yard of her and stopped, seemed his legs refused to take him any closer. The room sparkled with light from the windows, nothing haunted or frightening about it, as he had imagined it. He could have been standing in some resort hotel, somewhere far and away. "Look, Weird Sister, I got this little problem and I was wondering—"

"Well, Percy Terrell," she said, taking a pipe out of her pocket. "I ain't heard you call me that since 1952." She scooped and worked the pipe in a leather pouch full of tobacco.

Percy's eyes grew wide and even amused. "What?" He even grinned, involuntarily, so taken aback was he. " 'Weird Sister'? You remember the last time I called you that? Hell, I ain't talked to you in over thirty years."

Tabitha drew on the pipe, squinting in the cloud of sweet fog, and, blowing out the match, giving him a look as if to say, *Boy, you don't know your asshole from your mouth, do you?* said, "I made it up the year."

"Look," Percy said, after clearing his throat, feeling more than a little betrayed, more than a little stupid, more than a little . . . "Look, I ain't got time for this. I need—"

"Know what you need. Why you came here. Answer's no."

"Huh?"

"Can't do nothing for you."

"Wait a minute, What you mean, you 'know'?"

"Want to get rid of that damn hog a yourn, don't you?"

"Can you?"

"Oh, I can." Tabitha stopped and blew out a long stream of smoke, like a ghost's train, and looked upon him vaguely with pity that quickly transformed into scorn. "But you ain't gone be willing to do what you got to do to get rid of him. So why waste my time? Can't help you." She turned to the window, clearly having said all she would say.

Percy felt his face go red. When had someone last told him flat out no? No song, no dance? Refused him anything? After he had done such a thing as to actually come to this freakish old colored bitch for help, after . . . He stood there staring at this woman who had dismissed him so rudely, and it never once occurred to him that he might plead, beg, pour out his heart, that he might say *please*. He just got angrier, hotter, redder. Finding his voice, he finally said, shaking, "Well, why don't you just go right on to hell then, you crazy witch. You just crazy. Ain't a bit a nothing to that old foolishness you preach. Just a old charlatan. You just go right on to hell."

He watched himself storm out of the old house, wanting to break something, wanting to burn the entire abomination to the ground, vowing to himself that he'd break that old witch one day. So twisted with hate and malice and anger was he that he couldn't even frame his own thoughts, at that moment, so inarticulate with rage, such a rejected little boy that he almost came to tears. And, indeed, at the wheel of his truck, with the hog sitting quietly, peacefully beside him, as he drove down and away from the old house, the unfamiliar sting and pain and torment began moistening his cheek, and he did.

By the time he reached home, twilight had darkened past dusk, and, it being a Saturday night, Rose had already left for bridge and wouldn't be back until after eleven, and he simply wanted to forget this whole business, to forget the hog, forget the feeling the mystery of the hog precipitated within him, to forget how helpless and hopeless he was feeling. He locked himself in his study and snapped on the TV and popped *The Outlaw Josey Wales* into the VCR and opened a fresh bottle of his old friend John Daniel's, and took two enormous swigs before pouring four fingers neatly into a tumbler. He kicked off his shoes and loosened his belt and flopped back on the couch, before the flickering images of a West that never existed, concentrating intensely on the testosterone-deluded fantasy, and drank and drank. He had stopped drinking so much—well, during the week, now only on Fridays and Saturdays . . . except on special occasions; and he had stopped getting truly drunk . . . except on special occasions—but tonight that was exactly what he wanted, craved, he needed to erase, expunge, he lusted after what the bottle never failed to supply: power and ease and good feelings; he wanted to revisit the sweet veil of haze and be-bothered nothingness and the viscous warmth and head-fuzziness; he wanted to be released from tax codes and stupid children and orders and poultry and stocks and marriage, from maleness and the tug of gravity on his growing belly, to be released from the gray hair that he refused to dye out of a vanity stronger than fear and the red splotches and burst veins that would never vanish from his face and that signaled the end, years ago, of his virility and machismo energy; to be released from the memories of that once-youth, of his escapades and all the trouble his penis had seen and caused; away from memories of hunting and dancing and tomfoolery: released, yes, from the hog and all it seemed to signify. Percy drank. And drank. He swilled and slurped, he guzzled and gobbled, with a ferocious abandon, and with the swallowing, at his lips, and the fuzzy now-hum of his brain, somewhere in the amber liquid of the bottle, somewhere behind the black label, enlivened by the light of the TV screen, he saw his father, that old demon, with his big black hat with the huge brim, looking down upon his son with contempt. And Percy didn't want to see his father, never ever again, knew he was better than his father, could never be like his father, was a human-being person unlike his father, an evil, freak of nature, yes, he built it all up from nothing, yes, he started it, murdered for it, stole and beat for it, that sonofabitch, and left Percy with the blood, but Percy had, had—no, he didn't want to think of Malcolm, so he drank, and drank some more, the fire in his belly now outstepped by the fire in his brain, he willed himself to stop seeing Malcolm, and, stumbling up and over, switched off the VCR and turned on the CD player and fell back on the sofa to the measured twangs and lonesome chords of Hank Williams, "Goodbye Joe, me gotta go . . ." and sang with Hank (hell, Malcolm never could sing, never sang, never would sing), laughing and goofy in the clouds and fumes of mash and Benedict, Benedictine, and the deluged fretted in Antioch, O Antioch, where the glad rags had orgies of ragout in Shiloh, O, by the door of Doomsday, yes, in Berlin where superior werewolves were sailors with head colds who lost the compasses in that distance that joint— what was its name?—of pus-filled pushovers who submit, submit, wogs and Zeus, yes, zilch, in shampoo, Zimbabwe! Gomorrah! Dye. Die . . .

And somewhere, somehere, somethere, in the misfiring synapses and purple blaze of effluvium that had seized his brain and body, somewhere just before passing out, Percy saw his hog sitting there by him, by the couch, and felt a little love in his heart for this friend of his, and reached out to pet him, and, forgetting he held a glass, dropped it, and his mind went to black.

The next morning, the head deacon and chairman of the board of trustees of St. Thomas Aquinas Presbyterian Church of Tims Creek, Percival Malcolm Terrell, sat on the second pew along with the rest of the congregation, with a hangover that rivaled the worst hangovers of his youth— though he knew from half a century of heavy drinking that a bad hangover makes its own history. Percy felt he was indeed still drunk, for as he rose at seven after Rose banged and banged on the door to his sanctum sanctorum for him to get up and get ready for church, and as he washed and shaved and squirted drops of Visine into his eyes, and picked at his breakfast and drank four cups of coffee, the world was still tinged with a colorless aura, things were enveloped yet within a nimbus of gauze and otherness, and though he felt sick to his stomach, the alcohol had provided, at least for a spell and at a cost, a distraction from his mental confusion, had given his mind a respite from the hog, which was nowhere to be seen.

Now he sat before Pastor Bergen, who could not preach to save his life, droning on and on about the faith of Zacchaeus up a tree, now he was playing the role he had part inherited and part worked for, a role so old it was capacious and well worn and comfortable, and took so little effort he had barely to think upon it to be it: he was it: he was king of his little fiefdom of mills and poultry plants and fields and social rungs, richer than most men dared hoped to be, and feared, respected, paid homage unto. Why on earth should he worry about anything other than cancer and taxes? And as Bergen drew thankfully near the end of his overlong sermon, Percy felt more than a little better and the nausea seem to abate and his mind to clear a bit and he thought of the football game he would cheer on after dinner with the kids and he realized he had not even thought of the hog all morning. As the colored light from the stained-glass windows played against the pristine whiteness of the church walls, Percy smiled to himself.

The commotion started as a low-level rumble. Whispering turned to loud talk, and somebody said, "Git it, Frank!" By the time the minister stopped in mid-sentence and stared, Percy could hear people standing, some laughing, some angry, "How'd it get in here?" and before Percy could turn all the way around, he heard a grunt at his side: there was his old friend, his familiar, his companion and seeming advocate, his own and only hog. But the thing that Percy's mind latched onto was the fact that everyone saw the hog! Percy felt released. Yet, oddly enough, the hog had stopped by his side, as if to point a finger, or a snout, at him.

"What?" Percy hollered at the hog. *"What do you want from me?"*

With that, the hog gave out its signature bellow and rushed toward the pulpit, around to the side and up toward the Reverend Paul Bergen. The men in the front pews, unwieldy in their Sunday-go-to-meeting best, all jumped to their feet, and the pastor let out a girlish yelp, gathered up his robe like a woman's frock, and ran, being chased by this boar hog, its oversized genitalia jangling betwixt its legs, its big ears flapping like the wings of a bat, its mouth wide and frothing. As the men of the church chased after the hog, and the women screamed, and the children laughed with unbridled wildness, Percy was just thankful and amazed that everyone, everyone, could see the hog, at last, at long last, and he felt that the whole six-week ordeal was coming to some end, was about to affix itself to a clear and final meaning.

The men tried in utter vain to grab the hog, but it proved too ornery, too sly, and kept slipping between their legs, knocking them over and down, for it was, indeed, a very large hog. At one point it actually bit Pernell Roberts on the hand, which made Pernell cuss ("Goddamnit!") in church, though no one bothered to scold him, for at that instant the renegade swine chomped down on the edge of tablecloth on the communion table and backed up, pulling the Eucharist, the silver pitchers full of grape juice, the little glasses, the silver platters containing wafers, all crashing, clattering, tumbling down with a metal thunk and splatter. Momentarily everyone stopped, the men, the pastor, the women, the children, Percy, the hog, stopped, witnessing the spectacle as if, in that brief wrinkle in time, it revealed some clarity, some hidden codeology in this bedlam. But the hog brought an end to that sober oasis of reflection when it moved its head, with its bedazzling speed, toward

Percy and grunted derisively, giving otherworldly language to its own unquestionably blasphemous actions, and with equal speed dashed down the aisle toward the door.

Without thinking, Percy moved in front of the great mass of pork, to stop it, calling out, "Whoa!" as one would to an intelligent, malevolent, comprehending entity. "Stop," he cried. But the hog didn't stop, poking its behemoth head between Percy's spread thighs and lifting him astride its wide neck, and continuing down the way, Percy being carted along and atop, backwards, yelling, through the throng of the agitated congregation. At the threshold of the church Percy fell off, unceremoniously and painfully, and the hog galloped away.

Percy scrambled to his feet, and, feeling somehow personally responsible, and even possessive, he gave chase, running down the side of North Carolina Highway 50, after that great boar hog, which had just disrupted the services of St. Thomas Aquinas Presbyterian Church beyond conceivable imagination. Running, Percy didn't even give a second thought to the fact that they were running, unmistakably, inevitably, to his own home.

Though Percy's house was less than a mile from the church, he stood in the doorway breathless, his heart pounding dangerously, sweat pouring copiously down his face, for he had not run this far, or this fast, in years, not to mention the nausea he had been battling all morning. He tugged off his tie and doffed his coat to the floor, and stalked to his study. His mind was a red place, a hot place, a place of brimstone and vengeance; he was not simply angry with a thing, but with a confounding circumstance, a situation, a tangle of happenstance and botheration. He knew there was one way to get rid of it all, a way that had never clearly presented itself before, since the creature had never acted so hatefully. Percy marched into his study and, perhaps due to the anger and the urgent need to strike out at something, broke the glass of his gun rack with his elbow and a rebel yell, rather than waste time looking for the key, which was in his pocket. He reached for the old elephant gun he had used once in Africa in 1952, and not since, though he had kept it clean religiously. He loaded the shells, feeling the ungodly size of them in his hands, himself feeling suddenly potent with each insertion, wondering to himself why he had not done this most obvious of things long before.

Percy raised his head to the door, and, as he knew it would be, there stood his hog, his hog, insolent, inquisitive, mocking. Percy sneered at the beast, thinking and then saying out loud, for none would appreciate this outsized drama more than he, like some celluloid cowboy show in his brain: "End of the line, fella."

Percy had the hog in his sights, right between the eyes. They both stood there, stock-still for a period of time Percy could not easily name. Percy and the hog. The hog and Percy. The hog did not move, and by and by, Percy thought: *What a magnificent creature.* Unaccountably he began to tremble and inadvertently he peered into the hog's eyes, into the depth of them, perhaps toward the soul of it; and to Percy it seemed the hog did the same to him. Percy's trembling increased and a feeling began to wash over him and into him, and Percy began to feel puny. Naked. Ashamed. Just as he had at that moment when he discovered that his penis was not the largest in creation and that the juice of his testicles would neither save nor solve humanity; neither save nor solve himself; that all he had, he and his father had stolen and robbed for, and that he had no right to any of it; that he was next to nothing, and that the mask of his flesh, once glorious, now wrinkling and withering, would in time be dust and ash, and that he was really not very, very much at all, not even as valuable as a hog. Percy began to cry. He could not shoot. He would not shoot. He should not shoot. He understood in this moment of pregnant possibility, this showdown, this climax of it all, what the hog was. And in a moment of quiescence and acquiescence, Percival Malcolm Terrell let it all go, let the gun slip from his hands, and slumped to the floor of his study, a feeling like exhaustion settling into his bones. The great boar hog, on scuffling hooves, came rushing, and leapt, springing impossibly, up, into the air, and Percy, in chilled fright, watched as the mammoth creature sailed, like a gargantuan football, toward him; and he could only shield his face with his hands, and quake.

A few instants later he heard Rose run into the house, calling, "Percy, are you all right? My God, Percy!" He slowly uncovered his face to see only the open window, a breeze gently troubling the sheer curtains inward, barely a billow. Percy continued to sob, though the sob had altered in its tenor and meaning: now the sob was a sweet, deep, wonderful and profound sob, his body shaking, snot running down his nose. Rose walked into the room, but Percy did not really see her or hear her, so intent was he upon this newfound and peaceful feeling. He felt just like that bird in the old Hank Williams song, the one too blue to fly, and tried to mouth, "Hear that lonesome whippoorwill," but only the mumblings of a child emerged. Lonesome, oh so lonesome.

God's Gonna
Trouble the Water

or,

Where Is
Marisol?

for Mrs. B.

Mrs. Streeter was down in Barbados being chased by monkeys when the storm struck.

Her son, Aaron, had sent her on vacation with his daughter, Desiree. The two had been returning from a trip to the caverns—the spooky Harrison's Cave with its stone pillars hanging down and sticking straight up—when the hooligans showed up, green monkeys, but a brownish gray they were, with white furry breasts and menacing red eyes.

Desiree had found it amusing at first, but at eighty-two the widow wondered about the promises her son had made about the recuperative powers of Caribbean sun and ocean breezes. As she listened to the monkeys hooting and howling and grunting, she felt it might be better for her to be at home tending her okra and string beans.

Desiree, only eighteen, a college student at Spelman, pushed her scooter faster than the monkeys ran. (Mrs. Street had a problematic back and couldn't do a lot of long-distance walking.) The mischievous bandits seemed to have no objective, no reason, just causing trouble. But this did not inspire solace. Desiree kept just ahead of the troop, and made it back to the shuttle safely, and helped her grandmother climb aboard.

"I was so scared, Nana."

"I was worried, child. I'm glad I wasn't on foot. Lord have mercy."

"Nobody told me there would be monkeys!"

When they got back to the resort, murmurs were going on all about the lobby from other guests, mostly Americans. Clearly something was afoot. Two hurricanes were in the forecast: one headed to Barbados, and one headed for the North Carolina coast. Home.

IN TRUTH the Barbadian encounter with wind and rain felt like a mere thunderstorm—it came and went the next night in a hurry, leaving little damage—but the news regarding the coast was not so benign. Category 5, they were predicting. The governor was calling for evacuations. It looked like Mrs. Streeter would not be going home, but that is where she longed to be, deep in her heart, floods and wind be damned.

Back to the States two days later, Aaron met them at Dulles International Airport, and insisted his mother stay with him until conditions at home were safe. His town house was in Alexandria, and the sun was shining. Hard to imagine how different things were at that moment back in Tims Creek, where the storm was supposed to hit land the next morning. "Girl, it's been raining hard for the last two days straight, and I mean a hard rain too. All the creeks and rivers are about to spill over." Mrs. Streeter had been on the phone with her sister back in Tims Creek several times each day.

"Are y'all gonna leave?"

"No, child. Clay says we'll be just fine. You remember in that last flood we stayed high and dry, and the water got pretty high that time around town in the lower spots. So we're gonna take our chances."

Mrs. Streeter's days were largely CNN and the Weather Channel and talking on the phone, from the time Aaron left for work until he returned. Some days she'd cook his favorite meals—her special spaghetti, smothered chicken, oxtail soup—it was nice that he did all the shopping. Or, he would take her out to a nice restaurant. She really enjoyed that place called Busboys and Poets. They had some really nice shrimp and grits, and she enjoyed their Cobb salad. These young folk today sure wore their hair in some peculiar styles and colors.

After a week she worried more and more about home. They said miles and miles of Interstate 40 were still covered by water. Her sister told her their power had been out all week. "And you know that great big oak tree in front of Mama's house? Girl, it snapped in two. It blocked the road for three days before they could get to it and haul it out of the way." That tree was truly massive, too tall to climb, probably close to two hundred years old. It had been there when her great-grandfather built the house. Mrs. Streeter fondly remembered playing on its great gnarled roots as a girl. Something twanged at the bottom of her heart. Now she was even more worried about her vegetable garden, a thing in which she took enormous pleasure and spent a lot of time and effort cultivating. Her doctor had once told her, her longevity and robust health—even when considering the back problems and mobility—were surely aided by her daily exertions in that great big plot of earth, a third of an acre large.

She had been trying for days to reach the woman who helped her out a few days a week. But she could get no answer. This silence made her worry all the more.

After her back operation, Aaron wanted to pay someone to come help with cleaning and various chores around the house. Mrs. Streeter insisted she would be fine on her own, but Aaron insisted. Some of his high school buddies recommended Marisol Cifuentes, a pleasant dark-eyed woman in her mid-twenties with a gentle manner. who often brought her two girls along, Lourdes, age eight, and Ines, age six. Her husband Simitrio worked as a logger in the swamps. He ran heavy sawing equipment. They lived in a trailer park about eight miles away.

In time Mrs. Streeter grew to like Marisol, and looked forward to seeing the girls, who would sit and watch television with her, color in their coloring books, or fiddle with their phones. She remembered the day Ines asked her sister, "Can you itch my scratch for me?" and how it made her laugh out loud. Surely they had gotten out in time. God knows. That trailer park was awfully close to the Chinquapin River.

FINALLY, EIGHT DAYS after returning to the States, she caught a plane home. Her sister had told her the coast was clear, the water had largely gone. Her brother-in-law Clay picked her up at the Raleigh-Durham airport. She had already been filled with something like dread, though darker, about what she would find at home. Once she'd pulled off the interstate into York County and driving down the country roads to Tims Creek, the dread grew thicker. The roadsides along the way, in front of a great many houses, were littered with piles and piles of ruined and soggy Sheetrock, water-logged mattresses, useless refrigerators and other appliances, and all manner of refuse. Such a sight made a person wonder about the hours of work done and to be done.

Her mood lightened a little when Clay turned into the driveway. The brick ranch-style house her husband had built for them back in 1972 was standing proud, the flood had not budged it. Now for the insides. Clay came with her.

As soon as she opened the garage, the foulest odor she had ever smelled greeted her. It smelled like death itself: a profusion of fish and shrimp, spoiled. Even closed, the two freezers kept in the garage reeked from the spoilage. Also gone were all the corn and okra and butter beans and squash and collards and cabbage she had grown, not to mention the blueberries and pears and peaches and sweet potatoes she had frozen for pies. The water did not enter; the lack of power had struck. "Damn." The widow rarely swore, if ever, but this was one of those occasions.

Clay took her luggage to her room. The lights were back on. The water was running. She inspected the refrigerator, which was of course in bad shape, as expected. Otherwise the house seemed intact.

As for the garden, it had indeed become a total loss. All the plants had drowned. The water had caused most of the rows to erode and melt away. There was little green left, mostly yellow and brown and black. The sweet potatoes had commenced to rot. She knew it would be weeks before the ground would be dry enough for replanting. She let out a frustrated sigh. "Jesus help me."

———

AFTER MANY hours on the phone, arranging for someone to come help her clean the freezer and the garage in the morning, filling in Aaron and Desiree, and catching up with her sister and all the news around town, she finally went to bed in her own bed for the first time in two weeks, and she slept like the proverbial baby.

Mrs. Streeter woke to the sound of a vacuum cleaner, and the sounds of little girls' laughter. Marisol! She let herself in. She's okay. Mrs. Street took her time but was eager to see mother and children and to tell her all about her trip and to hear about the storm and how they fared.

But when she rounded the corner down the hall into the family room, she was met by no vacuum cleaner, no little girls, no mother. The room was silent and empty, save for the light pooling in through the sheer curtains.

The sense of bewilderment in her breast was a thing akin to her dead garden out back. How could she imagine such a thing? Why? It took two cups of decaf coffee and the entire *Today* show to get her relaxed finally.

One of her cousins, Noreen, showed up to help her empty and clean the stinky freezer, and to mop up the leakage that had spread all over the two-car expanse. This was a nauseating task, full of elbow grease and discarded once-deliciousness. It took several cleanings to get rid of the stench, which somehow lingered faintly for days.

STILL NO word from Marisol. No one was answering her cell. The widow decided to take a drive. The small community where the trailer park was located was known locally as Scuffletown. No one she spoke with knew how the tiny huddle of farms and homes had fared, being so low and so close to the river. Many trees had toppled over in the woods on either side of the road. As she approached, she witnessed more and more damage. When she got there, she saw trailers off their mounts, floated into odd and strange configurations; some overturned; many light poles down and wires downed and exposed. Surely the Cifuenteses got out. Surely they were okay. Lord knows.

On the way back home, Mrs. Streeter stopped by the local shop, La Michoacanita Tienda Mexicana—"the getting place" for the Spanish folk. She had never set foot in there; for some reason she just didn't feel comfortable going in there. She reckoned they didn't sell anything she couldn't get at the IGA or the local Dollar General. But she knew it had a particular reputation among the local folk for its extra-thick pork chops. Her sister swore by them. ("I mean to tell you, it's the best pork I've ever put in my mouth. They say he buys his hogs whole from a little farm over near Kinston. Talk like the farmer only feeds the pigs mostly on fruit. That's some sweet meat, girl. You hear me?")

The place looked to be like any other convenience store, except for the many colorful signs and banners advertising in Spanish, and all about were phone cards for sale, and even some cell phones. The place was quite orderly and kempt. She didn't know what she had expected.

"Hello," she said to the young woman behind the counter. "I'm looking for Marisol Cifuentes. Would you happen to know her? Or Simitrio Cifuentes or their children?"

The young woman, a girl really, shook her head no. "I'm sorry. I do not know this woman."

Mrs. Streeter briefly considered leaving a message or to ask for some other type of help but thought better of it. "Thank you."

After a pause the young woman said, "The owner, Mr. Garcia, he might know her. But he's in Greenville. His son is in the hospital. I don't know when he'll be back."

The widow thanked the young lady and returned to her car and went home.

WEEKS PASSED. Things got better, bit by bit, inch by inch. Eventually Mrs. Streeter was able to replant her garden with a few items, mostly cabbage and collards and mustard and kale. It being August, the growing season was going to be mighty short. It would start to frost in about six weeks. You could already sense fall coming.

The community slowly rebuilt. Very slowly. Many homes still remained gutted and vacant. Some stores had opened and restocked. The county and groups like the Red Cross and church associations were still showing up in trucks loaded with free bottled water and canned goods; one crusading minister was famous in eastern North Carolina for driving to the aid of hurricane victims with hammer, nail, and a strong back. Yet places nearer the coast were still impassable. Most of the schools had finally reopened after weeks. Wilmington was essentially an island, the governor said.

"DID YOU hear about Malcolm Terrell, Percy's son, you know the one with all them factory hog farms? You hear what happened at his walled-off country club and golf course? You know, that place over near Crosstown? . . . Well, you know he's built that big old house right smack plumb on the riverbanks, that place they call Biltmore East, with all that old expensive timber they found at the bottom of the river? I ain't never been in there, but folk talk about how it is some kinda fancy. A real palace like. Great big . . . Well the place flooded, and you know the hog lagoons with all that hog shit spilled over into the river, along with dead hogs from his farms. I was told when his mansion flooded, not only was the first floor filled with shit, but with dead hogs too! Now ain't that something? God don't like ugly, I'm telling you!"

A WEEK before Thanksgiving, Mrs. Streeter heard her doorbell. She wasn't expecting anyone at this time of day. It was the postman.

"Good morning, ma'am. This letter came for you. It's foreign. I didn't want to leave it in the mailbox. It looks important. I figured you'd want to see it right away."

She thanked the man. The letter in hand had a fancy, colorful stamp and the postmark read: Ciudad Juárez, Chihuahua.

Mrs. Streeter returned to her chair and opened the handwritten letter. The printing was very neat.

Dear Mrs. Vanessa Streeter,
My name is Sonya Ruiz. We never met, but I was the
elementary teacher of Marisol Cifuentes and I am a
friend of her family. I have known Marisol for most of
her life. You should know I was born in York County,
where my parents were migrant workers in the 1970s.
So I know your town. Some local church people took

pity on me and sponsored my education at East Car-
olina University. Despite my US citizenship, I decided
to return to Chihuahua to care for my ailing mother in
1990 and decided to stay. In any case, I wanted you to
know this. During the hurricane two months ago, Mari-
sol's little girl was lost in the flood. Marisol and Simitrio
and Ines survived, but Marisol was heartbroken, as you
can imagine. She returned to Chihuahua with the aid
of a Mr. Ramon Garcia, who I understand runs a local
grocery store in your town. Marisol and Ines made
the trip okay. She came to see me after she arrived.
Things were quite fine, though she was sad, as you can
understand. She spoke very well of you and said you
were a very kind lady. Two weeks after returning home,
something very bad happened. As you no doubt have
heard, there are some very wicked men in our province,
men who always wish to get their way, no matter what
they must do. Marisol's younger brother, Jaime, was
kidnapped by one of these men and the family could not
pay the ransom. The entire family has been missing for
two weeks. I found your address among Marisol's things
at her mother's house. I thought you should know. I will
certainly contact you if I get word of their whereabouts
and what has become of them. I pray to God that they
remain safe. I understand you are a woman of faith.
Please pray for them as well.

> *Very Sincerely yours,*
> *Sonya Ruiz*
> *Ciudad Juárez*